3 0063 00240 4772

Main   Jan 2017

Jezebel's Revenge

DAVENPORT PUBLIC LIBRARY
321 MAIN STREET
DAVENPORT, IOWA 52801-1490

a novel by

Jacquelin Thomas

Sapphire
Books

Raleigh, North Carolina

Jezebel's Revenge © 2016 by Jacquelin Thomas

Sapphire Books

ISBN: 978-1533558596

All rights reserved. No part of this book may be reproduced in any form or by any means including electronic, mechanical or photocopying or stored in a retrieval system without permission in writing from the publisher except by a reviewer who may quote brief passages to be included in a review.

Sapphire Books trade printing. Manufactured and Printed in the United States of America

If you purchased this book without a cover, you should be aware that this book is stolen property. It is reported as "unsold and destroyed" to the publisher, and neither the author nor the publisher has received any payment for this "stripped" book.

For My Readers

I hope it was worth the wait!

Prologue

London, United Kingdom

Natalia had finally found the man of her dreams, but she had no idea that she wouldn't get to enjoy her happily ever after for too much longer.

I'm going to destroy her.

Glancing around the exotic oasis pool area, she could appreciate why Natalia and her new husband chose the Hewitt Hotel for lodging during their honeymoon trip. The hotel itself was the ultimate in modern decadent luxury, each room had its own style inspired by other cultures with no expense spared. It was perfect for someone like her—a free spirit with a desire for serenity. She could only imagine that the honeymoon suite was the perfect love nest for newlyweds.

Slipping on sunglasses, she ran her fingers through her dark curly wig, and shifted her body position on one of the lounge chairs stationed by the pool.

Two chairs down, Natalia and her husband sat talking.

Every now and then, Natalia giggled like a young girl in love. She looked happy.

She watched in smug delight as Natalia, wearing a sexy black bikini, coerced her husband into the pool, then trained her gaze on them as they swam from one end to the other.

Enjoy this time together because your new husband will soon be a widower.

Chapter 1

"You killed him," Natalia Winters Anderson exclaimed. "Reina, why did you have to kill my husband?"

"I knew it would hurt you," she replied with a wicked laugh. Pulling out another syringe, she said, "But don't worry. You will soon be reunited with your beloved."

Natalia screamed.

"Honey, wake up…"

She opened her eyes. "D-Dean… oh, thank God… it was just a dream." Natalia sat up, propping her back against a stack of pillows. Quivering with fear, her body couldn't be stilled, not even by the warmth of his safe embrace.

"Sounds like you had more of a nightmare."

"It was," Natalia responded, sinking with relief against him "I thought she killed you. Reina was going to kill me, too."

"Honey, I'm never going to let that happen," Dean

assured her.

His touch was reassuring.

"I never meant to bring Reina on our honeymoon. I'm so sorry." Natalia wanted nothing more than to focus her attention on Dean and their life together. She resented feeling like a victim. This was not going to become her new normal, she determined.

Dean drew Natalia into the comfort of his arms. "You went through something traumatic, sweetheart. I understand, but just know that I will never let this woman get near you again."

She shuddered involuntarily.

"Are you cold?"

"No, I just got this weird feeling for a split second, then it was gone." She placed a kiss on Dean's lips. "I'm really sorry for waking you up."

An easy smile played at the corners of his mouth. "I know how you can make it up to me."

She broke into a grin. "How?"

Dean whispered in her ear.

As Natalia slipped out of the sheer, lacy gown she'd worn to bed, all thoughts of Reina vanished from her mind.

"I wish I could transport this suite back home with us," Natalia said, her gaze traveling slowly around the room, soaking up the lavish soft furnishings, glorious fabrics, and separate seating area with comfortable double sofas. "I love it here." They had been in London for two days and Natalia was already considering moving to the U.K. permanently. She wanted to be somewhere where she could finally feel completely safe. Their time here had been perfect until last night.

"Dean, you're so good to me," she murmured with a smile. "My life seems almost like a dream. At least, this is a good one."

"It's no dream, sweetheart. This is the real deal."

"How would you feel about moving here?" Natalia asked. "I really love London."

He gave her a sidelong glance. "Are you serious?"

She nodded. "I'm not sure I'll ever feel safe in Raleigh."

"London is nice, sweetheart, but do you really want to live here away from everyone we love?"

"I guess not." Natalia ran her fingers through her hair, still damp from her shower. "I would feel better if Reina were locked up behind bars, but she's not. Dean, she could be anywhere and that's what really scares me. I hate feeling so vulnerable."

"She will slip up one day, sweetheart." Dean kissed her cheek. "She's not here in London, so you can relax. We're on our honeymoon."

Natalia smiled, tightening the belt on the soft, plush robe supplied by the hotel. "You're right." She changed the subject by asking, "What do you want for breakfast? Continental or a full English breakfast?" Natalia stuck her feet into a pair of plush slippers.

Dean smiled. "I don't know about you, but I worked up an appetite this morning."

She laughed. "Full breakfast, it is…"

"I'm going to take a shower."

"I'll order the food," Natalia said, admiring her husband's wide shoulders and large biceps.

He planted a kiss on her forehead before padding barefoot across the room.

Natalia placed a call to room service before walking over to the huge window, looking out at the urban playground of London bursting with life. The city was filled with world-class restaurants, theaters and museums.

The June weather was perfect with no rain, a welcomed change from the first two days. After breakfast, she and Dean were going to take their first tour on a double-decker tour bus around the city.

Her gaze dropped down to her gleaming wedding ring. She was married to a wonderful man; someone who loved her unconditionally. If only she could forget everything that Reina did to her.

"I'm not going to let her win," she whispered. "I'm trusting you Lord to protect me and my husband."

"Honey, you okay?" Dean asked.

A soft gasp escaped her. Natalia wasn't aware that he had entered the room.

She turned around, facing him. "I'm fine. How was your shower?"

"Great."

"Breakfast should be arriving shortly," she stated.

Natalia turned her attention back to the view of London before her. "It really is gorgeous here."

Dean joined her.

The feel of his hand stroking her back was pure bliss. Natalia turned to look at him. "This means a lot—you bringing me to London. It was sweet of you to remember that my daddy and I had planned to come here before he died. Each year, we traveled abroad to a different country."

His arms pulled her into a close embrace. "I know

9

how much you miss your father."

A knock on the door interrupted their conversation.

Dean crossed the floor in quick strides to let the waiter enter with their breakfast.

Natalia joined him at the table minutes later. "The food smells delicious." She lifted the cover to reveal scrambled eggs, sausage, bacon, mushrooms, baked beans and toast.

Seated across from her, Dean said a short prayer of thanks.

"Beans for breakfast," she murmured, "I don't know if I'm ready for that."

Dean chuckled. "They're good."

"I think you'll eat anything for breakfast." Natalia eyed her husband with love and affection.

The time after losing her father had not been a happy one for her—until she met Dean. He was a good man and she was confident of his love for her.

"You've barely touched your food."

Dean's voice drew Natalia out of her musings. "I was just thinking how much I love you. I'm excited about starting our life together. You won't regret your decision to marry me. Starting now no more thoughts of Reina."

He smiled. "I'm glad to hear it. We can't live the rest of our lives worried if someone is hiding in the shadows. That woman is crazy if she returns to Raleigh—the police will be looking for her, but even if she does… all I can say is that she'll be sorry. I will do whatever I have to do to protect you."

"I feel very safe with you."

"Good. Now eat your breakfast before it gets cold. We have a lot on our itinerary today."

Chapter 2

Jessica Campana aka Reina Cannon, slipped on a pair of dark sunglasses as she made her way through the London airport. She ran her fingers through her soft, brown curls, which flattered her olive-green eye color, thanks to her recent iris implant surgery three weeks ago in Tunisia.

She was finally heading home to North Carolina. Her plan was to fly directly to Raleigh until she read Natalia's wedding blog and found that she and her new husband had chosen London for their honeymoon. Jessica would never understand why people put so much of their personal business on Facebook and other social media sites.

As far as she was concerned, Natalia didn't deserve one ounce of happiness. She had inserted herself into Jessica's life—*big mistake.*

Now I'm going to make her regret the day she ever crossed me.

But Natalia wasn't the only one in her sights. She

planned to exact payback from Mary Ellen Reed as well. That nosy witch had been nothing but a headache to Jessica. Maybe once she was out of Holt's life, he would finally welcome his big sister into the family.

Jessica spent her time away thinking about revenge. It fueled her desire to return to the states and she was well prepared. Her features had been altered by surgery so that she would not be easily recognized. She was elated by the prospect of tormenting those who deserved it.

She had come to London to study her intended victim. Jessica briefly considered killing Natalia while she was on her honeymoon, but changed her mind. It would be too risky for one and two, the smitten new wife was always glued to her husband.

Jessica checked her watch. Her flight was leaving in another hour.

She stopped at an eatery near her gate. "I'd like a chef salad please."

Her cell phone rang and a familiar face popped up on the screen.

"Clayton, I was going to call you as soon as I finished my salad. I'm trying to eat before I get on this plane."

"I can't wait to see you."

His words brought a smile to her lips. "I feel the same way. It's been a while, huh?"

"Almost eight months."

"Did you get the information I requested?" Jessica asked.

"Yes."

Powerful relief filled her. "They checked out of the hotel yesterday. They should be home anytime now."

"We'll talk when you get here. Have a safe flight, babe."

Jessica ended the call and laid her cell phone on the table. Her stomach growled as she picked up her fork. "I know..." she muttered under her breath.

While she ate, Jessica spotted a woman in the restaurant that reminded her of Gloria, the person who rescued her from death but condemned her to a life of hell. She was convinced there was a reason that Henry and Gloria Ricks could not have children of their own—God knew better.

Gloria was a nurse midwife who terminated unwanted pregnancies as a side business. Young Jessie Bell Holt was one of those girls. However, Jessie Belle's pregnancy was too advanced, so labor had to be induced, according to Gloria. After she had the baby, her mother took her home so that Jessie Belle could live out the rest of her life without the burden of young motherhood.

Jessica stuck a fork full of lettuce and tomato into her mouth. She chewed slowly.

She had been that innocent little infant—a child thrown away like a piece of garbage. Stuck with a living baby, Gloria took her home.

The woman was not the nurturing type, which left Jessica often wondering why she bothered to keep her at all.

Jessica endured years of physical and verbal abuse growing up. So much that she was taken out of school after teachers began questioning her many *accidents*. When Jessica found the courage to defend herself against Gloria, her father started hitting her.

She was fourteen when she learned the true story of her birth after declaring they were horrible parents. Gloria relished in telling Jessica how her real mother just walked out without a glance backwards.

"You're lucky to have us," Henry said. "We could've

just let you die in a garbage can somewhere."

Jessica often wished they had done just that, because after that, her life went from worse to unbearable.

Henry took her virginity two days later. Gloria was out on one of her late-night calls. She was asleep in her room when he burst through the door. Jessica tried to fight him off, but wasn't strong enough.

When it was over, he blamed her.

Jessica never said anything about what happened—not even when she found out she was pregnant. She hid her condition beneath oversized clothes until she could no longer escape Gloria's scrutiny.

In her fury, Gloria blamed Jessica for seducing Henry. She took the verbal beating without uttering a response. She was used to it.

Gloria loved to drink and she was a mean drunk. There were times when she would physically abuse the teen by hitting her or constantly reminding Jessica how she would never amount to anything.

"You can forget about school, missy. And you gonna have that baby naturally. Maybe the pain will be enough to keep them legs closed for a while… no good heifer," Gloria raged. "You nasty hoe… that's what you are… incest… I can't believe it…"

When Henry came home, the woman turned her wrath on him. He denied it at first, accusing his nephew, Clayton of being the father.

Gloria clearly didn't believe him.

Amid their heated argument, Jessica learned they were not her biological parents.

After the initial shock wore off, she felt a huge relief that her baby was not conceived with her father.

The next day, when Clayton showed up, Gloria demanded to know if he had ever had sex with Jessica. He was three years older than her and while Jessica felt there was a mutual attraction, they never crossed that line because they were supposed to be 'family.'

Clayton and Henry did not have the best of relationships, but it deteriorated to nothing after he discovered that his uncle had molested Jessica. He and Henry would've gone to blows had it not been for Gloria's intervention.

Jessica's son was stillborn and she was devastated. Clayton was there to comfort her, sealing the growing bond between them.

A few months later, Henry came to her room late one night. Unbeknownst to him, Clayton was hiding in the closet. He had no idea that his nephew had begun sneaking into Jessica's bedroom through the window.

When Henry tried to force himself on Jessica, Clayton burst out, attacking him with a knife.

Although stunned, she didn't react to the scene happening before her. Jessica stood there watching as Henry fell to the floor in a heap.

"He's dead," Clayton whispered. "I need to go get Lenox."

"Who's that?" she asked in a low voice.

"He's the guy I work for. He'll know what to do about this."

Jessica was relieved that Gloria was out. No doubt she'd call the police and blame her for the crime. She couldn't stay in her room any longer with a dead body on the floor, so she went into the dining room to wait for Clayton to return.

Jessica sat down at the table.

She did not have long to wait. Clayton returned with two guys that she assumed were drug dealers.

"Pack an overnight bag and y'all get out of here," the one who looked like he was in charge said, "go to this address. If anyone asks, tell 'um you was there all night."

Jessica assumed this was Lenox. She nodded and moved quickly, tossing clothing into her backpack.

They left the house to do as they had been instructed.

The next day, Jessica returned to a fire ravaged house, a host of firemen and the police. When she identified herself as Henry and Gloria's daughter, she was informed that her parents were dead.

The investigation was brief. Henry and Gloria's deaths were ruled accidental since they were both heavy smokers. Jessica and Clayton never talked about what happened afterward.

He found her a place to live and while she finished school and searched for her biological mother, Clayton climbed the ranks of selling drugs.

Because of what she'd been told, Jessica expected that her mother would welcome her long-lost daughter with open arms, but that was not the case.

Jessie Belle rejected her.

She checked her watch and finished off the rest of her salad. Flight 3421 would be boarding in twenty minutes. Jessica straightened herself with dignity as she made her way to the departure gate.

Raleigh, here I come.

Chapter 3

Chrissy Barton sat down at her desk. She had just come into the office after showing a couple of houses to a client. She turned on her computer. While waiting for it to boot up, Chrissy checked her voice messages.

She smoothed her auburn hair with her hand. It still amazed her how much her life had changed for the better. The journey from prostitution to dealing with being bipolar to becoming a Christian was her testimony, and now part of her ministry. She was not completely over what Chrissy considered her mommy issues, but the journals Jessie Belle left behind provided insight on the woman who rejected her. If only she could reach her twin sister.

The police wanted to question Reina regarding the deaths of a couple and an attempt on Natalia's life. Eight months had passed and no one had heard or seen her—it was almost as if she had simply vanished.

Time passed quickly as she worked. It was a few minutes after one and she was hungry, but needed to finish up one last contract before she left to grab something to eat.

"Hello Chrissy…"

Surprised, she glanced upward. "Traynor… How are you?"

"I'm fine," he responded with a small smile. "It's been a while since I heard from you."

"I know I promised to keep in touch." Chrissy made a slight gesture with her right hand toward the empty chair. "Please sit down." She had promised herself that she would not disrupt Traynor and Holt's lives—they had already dealt with enough of Jessie Belle's secrets.

"I'm not keeping you from anything, am I?"

She shook her head. "I was just about to grab something to eat."

"Perfect," Traynor responded. "I'd like to take you to lunch."

It was a nice gesture, but she felt uncomfortable with accepting his offer. "You don't have to do this."

"You are a part of my family, Chrissy. I want to get to know you, but more importantly, I'd like for you to meet your brother."

Traynor's words were like music to her, but she was not sure that Holt would feel the same way. "Does he know about me?"

"Yes," Traynor responded, "and Holt wants to meet you, Chrissy."

This can't be for real. Why would he want to meet me? I pushed his mother off a balcony. "I really don't want to interrupt his life or yours in any way."

"You won't be," he assured her. "Are you ready to connect with you brother? We don't want to rush you if you're not."

Chrissy considered his words for a moment before responding, "I think I'm ready to talk to him."

"What would you like to eat?"

"The Greek restaurant on the corner has great food."

Traynor smiled. "I've never tried Greek, but I'm all for trying something new."

"In that case, you have to have the whole experience. Do you mind if I order for you?"

"Not at all. I trust you."

Chrissy thought she detected laughter in his eyes. "Do you have any food allergies?"

"No."

"Do you eat meat?"

"I don't eat pork anymore and I'm trying to stay away from red meat, but it's a work in progress."

Chrissy laughed. "I understand. I have hamburger withdrawals from time to time—they are my weakness." Lowering her voice to a whisper, she said, "I've been known to frequent Cook-Out late at night."

"Shameful…"

More laughter.

Her initial misgivings evaporated. She enjoyed spending this time with Traynor. He was kind and went out of his way to make her feel comfortable. Jessie Belle had found a gem in her choice of a husband. Chrissy wanted to ask Traynor about their relationship, but decided this was not the right time.

He held the door to the restaurant open for her.

They were seated quickly as most of the lunch crowd came through between eleven and one o' clock.

One of the waiters walked over to take their drink order.

When he left, Chrissy announced, "I spoke to a group of former prostitutes last night. I shared my testimony."

"That's wonderful," Traynor said.

"It was a good feeling to be able to share all that God has done for me with those women. To give them hope for the future."

"Too many times, we allow our past to dictate our future—we need to be transparent at times because it helps others to hear testimonies and words of encouragement."

"I have another piece of news. Business has been great. In fact, I bought my first house last week and I'll be moving in this weekend."

"Congratulations," Traynor said with a grin. "Do you need any help?"

Chrissy shook her head. "Thanks for the offer, but I don't have much, so it's an easy move."

"You may not be my biological daughter, but I pray one day you will look to me as a father figure. Jessie Belle wasn't there for you but I intend to change that."

She leaned forward, asking, "Can I ask why? I don't expect you to clean up the mess she made. None of this is your fault, Traynor. It's not your responsibility to atone for her sins."

Their waiter returned with tall glasses of iced tea and water.

Chrissy gave him their order.

When he walked away, Traynor said, "The day I married your mother—she and I became one. She's gone now, but the bond she and I shared is still there, especially where you and Reina are concerned. Jessie Belle wronged you and I intend to make things right by being here for you both."

Her gaze traveled to his face, studying his expression. "I have to say; I've never met anyone like you. You are such an honorable man. It's very refreshing. I bet Holt is a lot like you."

"Only one way to find out."

Nervously, she moistened her lips. "Okay, but let me get moved into the house first. Can you believe it? I *own* a home. I didn't even have a house on my mind, but when I saw it—I knew it was for me."

"I'm very happy for you." The warmth of Traynor's smile echoed in his voice.

Their waiter returned, this time with salad and grilled pita.

"This looks delicious," Traynor said.

Chrissy's mouth curved into an unconscious smile. "It is. I love Greek salads."

Their meals arrived ten minutes later.

"This is the gyro kabab—it's a steak and lamb mixture. I figured this was the best way to introduce you to Greek food. We also have rice, hummus, grape leaves, and tabouli."

"What's this sauce?"

"Cucumber," Chrissy said. "It's good."

Traynor sampled his kabab. "Mmmm... this is delicious."

"The next time, you should try the lamb kabab."

"I might order it to go. I plan to be at the church late tonight."

Chrissy allowed herself to believe that she was enjoying a nice lunch with her father. She made a mental note to invite him to lunch one day soon. He was easy to be around. She never sensed any judgement whenever he looked or talked to her. She was having such a wonderful time with him that she hated for it end.

Later at her apartment, Chrissy swallowed a pill and then drank water to wash the medication down. Between the medication and therapy, she felt in control of her bipolar disorder. She was smart enough to know that there was no quick fix to managing the illness. It was something she would have to live with, and Chrissy was finally okay with it.

There was a time when she condemned herself for all the bad choices she had made in the past, but getting to know the Lord on a personal level changed all that for Chrissy. She found out for herself that He was truly a God of second chances.

She picked up an empty cardboard box and carried it into her bedroom.

Chrissy opened her drawer and began taking clothes out. In a few days, she would be in her house—the first real house she had ever lived in. Growing up, she never stayed in a place long enough to call it home. She went from one group home to another.

Then she met Jay. He was nice to her until he started pimping her out. Chrissy didn't mind at first, but then figured out she preferred working on her own. She left Georgia at the age of seventeen and traveled up to Maryland with another girl. This time she worked the streets without a pimp.

"Those days are long gone," she whispered.

Chrissy sealed the box and labeled it. She walked back to her living room, picked up another box and brought it back to the bedroom.

She was excited about moving into the new house.

She would finally have a place of her own—something she could finally call home.

❧

The next day, a nice-looking man strolled into Brown and Barton Realty. They exchanged a polite, simultaneous smile as she rose to her feet and walked around the desk. "I'm Chrissy Barton. What can I do to help you?"

"Aiden St. Paul," he responded. "I'm looking for a townhouse with an office and three bedrooms."

She liked a man who knew exactly what he wanted.

Up close, he was far more handsome than she initially thought. His complexion, the color of honey, was dotted with a light sprinkle of freckles and complimented his golden-brown gaze. Chrissy estimated his height to be around six feet four.

Clearing her throat, Chrissy walked over to her desk. "I can certainly help you with that. What area are you considering?"

"I work in North Raleigh. I've been here for about two weeks now, so I don't know much about the area."

She could feel him watching her as she made notes, but she pretended not to notice. "Do you want to be close to your job?"

"It doesn't matter," he responded. "As long as I'm near the beltline."

"Mr. St. Paul, there are some great townhomes in the North Raleigh area. I can show you a few if you'd like."

"Is it possible to see them today? I'll be leaving town tomorrow and won't be back until Sunday. I'm getting tired of living in a hotel."

"I don't have any appointments so I'm free. I'll just

print out some listings now."

"While you do that, I have a couple of phone calls I need to make. I'll be right outside."

She released a sigh of relief when Aiden left the office. "Girl, get it together," she whispered.

"You're acting like you've never seen a gorgeous man before."

Patty, her partner walked through the double doors, saying, "Chris, you should see the nice piece of chocolate standing out front. He is *fine*."

She laughed. "That is Mr. St. Paul. I'm helping him find a townhouse."

"Is he single?"

"I have no idea, Patty."

"It's a good thing I'm married, 'cause I'd be tempted to sample that man."

Chrissy's eyes widened in surprise. "I can't believe you just said that."

"C'mon Chris… don't you find him handsome?"

"I'm not blind."

"Girl, then you need to find out more about that brotha. You're driving him around, right?"

"It's his choice, Patty. You know that."

"That could be your future out there. I'm just saying… Girl, don't mess around and miss your blessing."

Chrissy laughed as she printed out several listings. She and Patty had been partners for about three months. They met in real estate class and became fast friends. After two months in the business, Chrissy sold a property which had netted her a three hundred-thousand-dollar commission. Around the same time, Patty contacted her about starting her own office. Patty had sold real estate previously in another state, but let her license lapse after she got pregnant with her first child. Her daughter was now school age and Patty was ready to get back into business. They worked well together and planned to add additional agents in the coming months.

She was able to set up three showings by the time Aiden walked through the doors once more. "Did we get lucky?"

Chrissy rose to her feet. "I have three I can show you this afternoon."

His smile was bright and infectious. "Great."

Patty walked from the back. "Hello, I'm Patty Brown."

"So you two are partners," he said. "Brown and Barton Real Estate."

"Yes we are." Chrissy picked up her tote. "You're welcome to ride with me or if you prefer, you can drive."

"Since I'm new to the city, it might be better if I ride with you."

"Patty, I'll give you a call when I'm on my way back to the office."

"I'll be right here," she responded.

Chrissy struck up a light conversation with Aiden as she drove to the first appointment. "Where are you from?"

"Orlando, Florida. I came up here to start a new position with Newton Pharmaceuticals."

"Raleigh is a great place to live," she said. "I love the change of seasons and the fact that it's metropolitan and kind of rural at the same time."

"I was impressed by everything I read on the Internet and in the relocation package."

She glanced over at him. "Is this how you found us?"
"Yes."

"The first place we're going to see is on Six Forks Road," Chrissy stated.

Aiden looked over the details of the property. "Looks nice from the photos."

"It's only five years old and one owner."

"Is this a large community?"

"Not really. Is that something you prefer?"

"I'm okay either way," Aiden said. "Eventually, I'll upgrade to something larger, and use the townhouse as rental property."

He's a planner. We have that in common, she thought.

Chrissy pulled up in front of the property and parked. "Here we are."

"It's nice," Aiden said when they were back in the car afterward. "But I'm not crazy about the location of the fireplace or the layout of the bedrooms. They are too close together."

"So you' prefer the have guest bedrooms on the opposite side of the master then?"

"Yes," he responded. "I don't have to have a fireplace, but if I do—I don't want one in a corner."

Chrissy kept a mental note of his preferences.

After viewing the second property, she asked, "What are your thoughts on this one?"

"Not really my style. The look is too European for me."

"We have one more to see. I think you'll really like this one."

"Are you from Raleigh, Chrissy?"

"I've been here a long time," she responded. "I grew up in Georgia."

Chrissy could feel the heat of his gaze on her. She'd caught Aiden staring at her a few times, although she pretended not to notice. She considered his interest as fleeting—nothing to take seriously.

She drove into a luxury townhome community.

"Nice neighborhood," Aiden said.

"This one is at the higher end of your price range." Chrissy parked her car. She had a good feeling about this.

They moved through the townhouse, going from room to room. "It's only been on the market for a week."

"It looks hardly lived in," Aiden said. "I really like this one. It has everything I want."

They entered the master bedroom.

Walking through the sitting area, they entered a large suite boasting two full-size walk-in closets with custom cabinets built in. Through another door, a master bathroom with its own Jacuzzi and separate walk-in shower as well as a sauna. The room also had its own private balcony.

"What's the square footage on this one?" he asked.

"Three thousand square feet." Chrissy paused a moment before continuing. "I'll let you continue looking around."

She stepped from the room and descended the stairs to the main level.

Chrissy didn't have to wait long.

"I've made a decision. I want this one," Aiden said when he joined her downstairs. "If the owner doesn't accept my offer, then we'll look at more homes."

"If you have some time, we can go back to my office to fill out the paperwork."

"I don't have any plans."

"Great."

"I'd like to take you out to dinner to celebrate," Aiden said as he held the door open for her.

They had just returned to her office.

Chrissy smiled. "You don't have to do that."

"It's just dinner. I'm not looking for anything more."

"Mr. St. Paul, I appreciate the thought, but really …" She searched for the right words to say.

"I'm sorry, I didn't mean to creep you out. I meant no harm."

"No harm done." She didn't make it a habit of going to dinner with her clients. However, if it had been a woman, Chrissy probably would've accepted the invitation. Her eyes traveled to where

Aiden sat filling out paperwork.

He wasn't wearing a wedding ring and he never mentioned a wife, but that didn't mean he didn't have one.

"Thank you, Chrissy for all of your help," Aiden said, handing the papers to her.

Smiling, she responded, "The pleasure is all mine. I'll give you a call as soon as I hear back from the other agent."

When he left, Patty said, "That man is all kinds of handsome."

"Yes, he is…"

"Did you find out if he's married?"

"According to his paperwork, he's not," Chrissy responded. "He asked me to have dinner with him."

"I hope you said yes."

"I didn't."

Patty shook her head. "Girl, what is wrong with you?"

"I want to keep this professional."

"Okay, so after you get your commission check—you better get that man."

Chrissy laughed.

The next morning when she arrived to work, she was

greeted by a bouquet of yellow roses. Chrissy read the card that was attached.

Since you wouldn't allow me to take you to dinner, please accept these roses as a token of my appreciation for your help in finding my new home.

Regards,
Aiden

"He isn't one to give up," Patty said. "I like that in a man."

Chrissy leaned over and sniffed the bouquet. "So do I."

Chapter 4

Clayton had arranged for a car service to pick Jessica up. The fact that he hadn't come himself piqued her interest. It meant that he had something special planned for her. He was the one person she could always count on. The only constant in her life.

She called him from the back of the shiny black SUV. "I should be there shortly."

"I hope you're hungry. I made dinner."

"I have really missed your cooking." Jessica settled back against the cool leather. "I'm so glad to be off that plane. I don't like long flights."

"First class wasn't comfortable?"

She detected a hint of humor in his voice and chuckled. "It didn't make the trip any shorter."

"I'll see you when you get here."

The thought of seeing Clayton again sent a tremor of excitement through her. She was thrilled that he'd agreed to move to Raleigh because she needed him close by. He was a calming force for her.

Jessica stared out of the window as they traveled down the 540 freeway. It was refreshing to see familiar sights.

The house was in the North Hills area of Raleigh. Clayton had sent her photographs, but she couldn't wait to see it in person. She had never lived in a house that defied her deepest desires.

The driver pulled up to a gate and waited for someone to allow them entrance.

She knew how much Clayton valued his privacy. The French country home sat away from the street, and was within walking distance of North Hills.

The gates opened.

Clayton was standing outside when the car pulled to a stop in front of the home. He greeted her with a kiss. "It's so good to see you, babe."

She wrapped her arms around him, feeling safe. "Thank you for everything."

"Jess, you know that I'm always here for you."

"Wow, look at you." It was obvious that his daily work-outs were paying off, because of his muscle-toned physique. He looked handsome, dressed in a suit that probably cost thousands. Once Clayton started making money, he traded in his *Levi* jeans for designer clothing. He possessed the look of a man who did not like getting his hands dirty. He was no longer Clayton Ricks; he was now Clayton Wallace, using his mother's maiden name.

He wasted no time in escorting her into the house.

"How do you like Raleigh so far?"

He chuckled. "It's not New York, that's for sure. It's okay though. I still have my operations back there and I'll be branching out here. I don't want to be away from you."

Jessica sucked in a breath as she entered the house. A foyer with a domed ceiling opened off the entrance, stunning with its arching beams and a sparkling chandelier the size of a compact car. Gray stone blended into ivory walls and golden baroque molding. A round table in the center held a floral display so colorful and striking that it dominated the entire room.

"I love this house," Jessica murmured. "The photos you sent me just don't do it justice."

"I told you… *I know you*, babe."

Hand on her hips, she scanned the interior of the living room with a critical eye. The couches, cream with a soft floral pattern. "Yes, you do."

She followed him through the huge dining room and into the gourmet kitchen. "Very nice." It was the most striking interior Jessica had ever seen.

Under a vaulted ceiling with heavy beams meeting in the middle sat an array of couches, two overstuffed chairs and a coffee table. Perching on a chair, Jessica eyed the huge aquarium against the wall in the family room. "I see not much has changed. You still have your reef collection. It's gotten much bigger I see."

"I have palythoa and zoanthids from all over the world."

Fingering the leaves of a nearby potted plant, Jessica smiled. "We've come a long way from that little hick town in Georgia."

"This is *our* home. No more trailers for us."

"I feel like I'm moving into a castle."

Clayton laughed. "Well, this one belongs to you. Babe, you don't have to lift your finger to do anything. We have a housekeeper."

Jessica shook her head. "No. I don't want anyone going through our personal things. I don't mind cleaning. It relaxes me."

"You sure about this? This house is over five thousand square feet."

"It's only you and me in here, sweetie. I don't think we will have to constantly clean all of the rooms."

"Okay. I'll get rid of Maria."

They settled down on a love seat.

"It's strange looking at you but seeing a different face."

Jessica smiled. "So what do you think?"

"You're still beautiful."

"But you're not really crazy about it."

"You're more than your outward appearance," Clayton stated.

"I couldn't come back here without changing my appearance. Wigs and contacts wasn't going to cut it."

He planted a kiss on her lips.

"If only Henry and Gloria could see us now."

"I would never let that man anywhere near us," Clayton stated.

"Why do you hate Henry so much?" Jessica asked. "And don't try to change the subject.

What happened between you two?"

"I knew the type of man that he was. Truth is, I never would've been around him if it wasn't for you."

"Did he…" she couldn't finish the thought.

"Not me," Clayton interjected. "He raped my mom— his own brother's wife. When my father confronted him.

Henry killed him."

Jessica gasped in shock. "He said that he thought it was a thief trying to break in. I remember that night. I was so scared."

"My dad went there to confront Henry. Mom and I was in the car and saw everything that happened."

"Did your mom tell the police about the rape?"

"No," Clayton said. "She thought it was her fault somehow. Mom wouldn't even tell them that Henry killed his brother intentionally."

"That's why you and Henry never got along," Jessica stated.

He gave a slight nod. "I wanted to protect you. I knew they weren't treating you right and I tried to get my mom to talk to Gloria, but she wouldn't. Henry came to our house one night, but I told him I'd kill him if he ever came back. It's the reason I joined the South Street Knights. I wanted to make sure my mom was protected from Henry."

"How come you never told me this?"

Clayton reached over and took her hand in his. "I hated thinking about him, much less talking about that piece of trash. My mom kept her rape bottled up inside her until she lost her mind. When she died, all I felt was relief."

He was impassioned when speaking about those years, prompting Jessica to respond, "You did your best to get her help."

"I felt bad committing her into an institution. I wanted so much to protect her."

"You were just a little boy, sweetheart. I have a better understanding now of why you always wanted me to stay at your house. I didn't back then because I didn't know... Gloria always said you had a crush on me—"

"I'm not a rapist," Clayton interjected stiffly. "She was the one married to a predator. Besides, I thought you were blood and I knew he'd come for you one day."

Jessica gave his hand a light squeeze. "Thank you for trying to look out for me. I used to think that God hated me and that's why he sent me to Gloria and Henry. I still don't understand why I had to suffer. Why couldn't I have normal parents—it's all I ever wanted."

"Honey, you don't need parents now. You have me—you've always had me. We may not be blood, but we will always be family. We can do whatever we want, Jess. I have more than enough money to live the lifestyle we've always dreamed of and forget the pain of our youth."

He kissed her. "I made good on my promise. I told you when we left Georgia that I would give you everything your heart desires. I can even give you a family if you'd let me."

"Clayton, you can't give me *my* family."

"I'm the only one that you will ever need," he said.

"Every time I think about Henry and Gloria; I feel such rage. I wish that I had been the one to make them pay. My face should've been the last one they ever saw."

Trust me, you were their last thought," Clayton stated. After a brief pause, he continued. "Jess, I want you to think about something. Is this woman worth it?"

"She knows too much about me. She made the mistake of reading my journal."

Clayton raised his gaze to hers. "You kept that diary?"

"Honey, there is nothing in it to incriminate you. I never even mentioned you by name. You know that."

"Oh yeah. You called me X whenever you wrote about me. You even said that one day you were going to be Mrs.

X."

Jessica laughed. "I can't believe you remember that."

"My offer still stands," he said. "We can be partners. Jess, you have a strong head for business."

"I've worked in your business and it's not for me, Clayton. Selling drugs is a dangerous business. I want no parts of it."

Clayton chuckled. "Says the woman who has no problem killing folk."

She gave a slight shrug. "People should mind their own business."

"I have several legitimate businesses of my own, Jess."

"So, are you saying that you don't sell drugs anymore or will not hesitate to take someone out if necessary?" she questioned.

"I head an organization that supplies narcotics and yes, I *will* kill but only if it's warranted."

"Okay, that's so much better."

"They may never accept you, babe. Why don't you give up this quest for revenge?" Clayton questioned. "Forget about those people. Marry me. We can live out our lives in luxury."

"You are the one who taught me that people should pay for the hurt they inflict on others."

"Don't you think that this implies to you as well?"

Jessica shook her head. "Actually no. I'm just handing out payback."

Clayton hated violence but did not hesitate to do whatever was necessary. He had built up a reputation of being silent but deadly.

"Two of my men are here," he announced. "They are staying in the guest house."

Jessica nodded.

"Tomorrow, I'm taking you shopping for a car. You can get whatever you want."

"Clayton, you don't have to do this. You grabbed my salons after they went into foreclosure.

I really appreciate that."

"So what are you going to do with them?"

"I'm not sure. Maybe we can get into the hair business."

Clayton shook his head. "No, I think you should sell. You do not need to have anything that will connect you to your past."

"That's fine. I'm tired of superficial women coming in and wanting to look like Beyoncé or Halle Berry when they should be asking for plastic surgery."

"You may not look like you anymore, but you're the same ol' Jess…"

"I'm different Clayton and I think you know it. The night Henry raped me… I changed. I vowed that no one else would ever victimize me again."

"Jess, you've taken this a step farther and you know it. Mike wanted to control you and look what happened. Then you decided to get rid of his wife."

"I didn't want to do it, Clayton, but she wouldn't leave me alone. She kept accusing me of murdering Mike. It was necessary to get rid of her."

"You were sloppy, Jess. Now you're wanted for two murders. If this Natalia suddenly dies, don't you think the police will put two and two together?"

"So I'm supposed to just let her live? She's the reason I'm a murder suspect."

"She dies and you are headed to death row," Clayton

said.

"So what am I supposed to do? Just give her a pass."

"No, but you can discredit her. Plant the stuff you used in Mike and Charlotte's death in her house and make an anonymous call to the police. Give them a reason to suspect her."

Jessica smiled. "I like it. I can ruin her life like she tried to ruin mine. In fact, I think it's time she and I became BFF's."

Clayton grinned. "That's my girl."

"I don't want to talk about any of this stuff anymore. I want to focus on just the two of us right now."

"It's been a while…" he murmured as he rose to his feet.

Jessica stood up and followed Clayton upstairs to the master bedroom.

In the room, he pulled her so close to his muscled chest that she could hardly tell where her body left off and his began. Jessica's hands slipped up behind his neck and she found herself pulling Clayton even closer.

"I missed you so much," she whispered.

He broke the kiss long enough to trail his lips down her neck.

Jessica stepped out of his embrace to remove her clothing. "You're about to make love to a new woman."

"Honey, it doesn't matter what you look like on the outside. Inside, our hearts beat as one. I would know you anywhere, Jess."

"I know I don't say it a lot, but I do love you."

He picked her up and carried her over to the bed. "You were always better at showing me."

After a round of making love, Jessica drifted off to

sleep.

Clayton woke her gently. "Babe, I made a bubble bath for you."

She smiled. "How long was I sleep?"

"About an hour."

Jessica sat up in bed. "You're already dressed." He had slipped on a pair of sweat pants with a matching top.

"I went downstairs to start dinner."

"What are you cooking?"

"Grilled salmon, rice pilaf and roasted corn."

She smiled. "Sounds delicious."

Jessica eased out of bed and padded barefoot across the floor to the bathroom.

"I'll be in the kitchen," Clayton announced.

Dressed in only a robe, Jessica came downstairs after her bath to find two men, hands clasped before them, eyes hidden behind sunglasses in the kitchen with Clayton. "Oh, I didn't know we had company."

"Come Sweetheart. I want you to meet Nikko and Miguel."

She tightened the belt around her robe. "Hello gentlemen."

"This is Jessica."

"Nice to meet you," they said in unison.

The one called Miguel looked as if he could've walked off a runway. Smooth golden brown complexion, square jaw, straight nose and full lips. His shoulders filled out the black shirt perfectly. The other, Nikko sported long dreadlocks, skin the color of coffee and a long scar that trailed down one cheek. He was an inch or two taller than Miguel, with broader shoulders and a muscled frame.

"As I mentioned earlier, Nikko and Miguel stay in

the guest house, but they have twenty-four access to the house," Clayton said.

"Not a problem. I see that you're busy so I'm going back upstairs."

"This won't take long. I'll join you in a few."

Jessica eased the door closed and walked up the spiral staircase to the second floor as if she were on an evening stroll.

She took a closer look at the bedroom suite. Opulence reigned in the bedroom, from the fine carpet to the sleek color scheme of emerald green and gold. Clayton had spared no expense in the plush make of the bedroom furniture. The walk-in closet was massive with a full dressing area within, complete with full-length mirrors and a couch.

She walked back to the sitting room where her luggage was placed. Jessica retrieved a maxi-length, strapless dress and put it on.

She wasn't surprised to find Nikko and Miguel still with Clayton when she returned to the kitchen.

"Are you two joining us for dinner?" Jessica asked.

"Yes, they are."

She smiled. "Great, so this will give me a chance to get to know you two."

Strolling into the kitchen, Jessica inquired. "What is everyone drinking?"

"Since this is a celebration of you coming home, grab the bottle of the 2012 Musigny Vieilles Vignes Grand Cru."

"Sounds expensive," she said.

"It's going to go perfect with the salmon."

Clayton owned a couple of restaurants and spent years learning about food preparation and wines. Jessica knew that his wine cellar boasted several expensive wines priced as high as five thousand dollars.

When dinner was ready, they all settled down in the dining room to eat.

She glanced over at Nikko. "How long have you worked for Clayton?"

"Going on three years," he responded with a thick accent.

"Where are you from?"

"From Hackney. I heard you were recently in London."

"Yes, I was," Jessica said. "I enjoyed my visit, but I'm glad to be home."

She took a sip of her wine. The flavor was powerful but still airy and refined. "This is delicious…"

"I figured you'd enjoy this one because the palate is smooth in texture and medium-bodied."

Jessica looked at him and chuckled. "If you say so. You're the only one at this table who is a wine connoisseur."

Nikko and Miguel nodded in agreement.

"I'm with Jessica," Miquel said. "All I know is that it tastes good."

"I know you're from New York," she told him. "You were a part of Clayton's old crew."

He nodded. "Clay saved my life. My allegiance is to him. I'ma always have his back."

Jessica sliced off a piece of her grilled salmon. "Loyalty is a good thing to possess."

"Nikko and Miquel… I trust them which is why I keep them close to me. Remember Slate? He's running my New York operations. He's been by my side since we were fifteen."

"I've always liked him."

Jessica took another sip of her wine. She was glad to be back in Raleigh and thrilled that Clayton had come to join her there when she asked. Her plans always seemed to work out better whenever he was around. He loved her. He would be loyal—of this she had no doubt. She needed someone she could trust—someone she could confide in. Clayton was the person who would step in and make sure she didn't make careless mistakes. But most importantly, he would kill for her if it became necessary.

❧

Jessica walked out of the bathroom and found Clayton, bare chested and barefoot, wearing a pair of black lounge pants that sat low on his hips in the sitting room. He was in excellent physical condition. "I need to get back in the gym. I can't have you looking better than me."

"We have a gym right here in the house."

She chuckled. "Of course you do. I forgot who I was talking to for a moment." Clayton loved working out. He said it gave him time to reflect as he physically challenged his body.

He gestured for her to sit. "Let's talk."

Jessica released a short sigh as she sat down next to Clayton.

"Babe, I'm serious. You can't be careless."

"I wasn't careless."

"Was it necessary to kill the preacher?" Clayton asked.

"He threatened to blame me for the embezzlement if I left him. Mike couldn't understand why I wanted to go back to Raleigh." She looked up at Clayton. "I didn't ask him to steal from the church. I just needed him to resign so that Traynor could be installed as pastor."

"Why did you get involved with him?"

Jessica didn't know if the question was out of concern or jealousy. "I figured it was easier to manipulate him if we were involved."

"You could've just set him up. He didn't need to be killed."

She shrugged. "There's nothing I can do about that now, Clayton. Mike's words would've carried more weight than mine, so I decided he had to go."

"And his wife?"

"That drug addict," Jessica muttered, "she figured out that I had something to do with her husband's death."

"Babe, she didn't have to die. You could've discredited her as well."

Jessica chewed her bottom lip, something she did whenever she was irritated. "It's easy for you to sit here and tell me what I should or shouldn't have done. *Where were you in all this*? I'll tell you. Chasing after that stupid model. I told you it would never work out. She left you for some NFL player."

Clayton's eyes narrowed. "I tried reaching out to you, but you wouldn't return my calls. I didn't hear from you until after you were on the run. I asked you to marry me … the next day, you're all packed up to leave."

"I wanted to find Jessie Belle. I didn't think it would take as long as it did, Clayton. I wanted to give her a chance to reclaim her daughter, but she didn't want that."

"This accident she had… did you push her over that balcony?"

Jessica shook her head. "It wasn't me. Jessie Belle had a lot of enemies, so we will never find out who the real culprit was."

Clayton wrapped an arm around her. "Jess, I know that the only reason you wanted to come back here is for revenge." His tone was coolly disapproving.

"Don't..." she said. "Let's not do this."

"We have to talk about this."

Her mood veered sharply to anger. "No, we don't. I am going to get payback and you can't stop me." Jessica picked up a pillow and threw it across the room.

"Calm down, Jess. I'm not your enemy."

She gave him a hostile stare. "Natalia broke into *my* house and she stole my journal. She inserted *herself* into my life."

Clayton remained silent.

"If anyone tried to get into your business, you would have them killed," Jessica said. "I know because I've been there when you gave the order."

"I only gave that order when there was no other option."

"This is my first night back. I don't want to debate or argue about this, Clayton. Can we table this discussion for tonight?"

"Sure."

Later that night, Jessica found it hard to sleep. Her mind was filled with images of Charlotte and the night she died.

"Why are you doing this to me? You wanted Michael and he chose you. Why didn't you just stay with him?"

"Mike and I were really good together in the beginning, but then he had this stupid idea to run away together and start over," Jessica stated. *"I didn't want to leave Raleigh."*

"Then why did you go?"

"I knew that it was for the best," she responded. "Mike would not leave unless I agreed to go with him."

"When you grew tired of him, what did you do?" Charlotte asked. "What did you do with the money? It wasn't found with him, so I can only assume that you took it."

Jessica smiled. "I'm not sure what you mean."

Her voice had drifted to almost a hushed whisper. "Did you kill him?"

"Charlotte, don't ask questions that you're not ready to hear the answer, because I won't lie to you."

Her eyes filled with tears. "Did you kill my husband?"

"I didn't want to spend the rest of my life tied down to a man I didn't love. I knew that Mike wasn't going to just let me go." Jessica met Charlotte's horrified gaze. "He loved me too much."

"Noooo..." Charlotte sank down on the sofa as if she could no longer stand.

Jessica stood to her feet and began pacing back and forth. "It's important that you understand that I wasn't trying to take your husband away from you, Charlotte. I simply wanted him out of the way. The church needed a new pastor. Disgracing Mike was the only way we would get one."

Charlotte stiffened in shock. "You did this so that you could get Pastor Deveraux to take over? You're sick!"

"No, that would be you, Charlotte." Jessica pulled a needle out of her pocket. "It's time to put an end to your suffering. You love Mike so much, now you can join him."

Hands up, Charlotte began backing out of the room. "Don't do this... I have a daughter... I won't tell anybody. Please just leave. I'm the only parent my little girl has left...."

"She'll be fine. I promise. Your mother will be there for Leah."

Charlotte reached for a nearby vase and flung it at Jessica, who for a moment was caught off-guard. Then, she laughed. "I'm just giving you what you want. Peace."

Screaming, Charlotte ran to the front door, but before she could get it open, Jessica grabbed her, and stuck the needle in her arm.

Although she tried to fend her off, Jessica was much stronger and whatever was in the syringe was already working.

Charlotte moaned. "Dear God… my baby…."

Jessica struggled but managed to get her on the sofa. "Go to sleep, Charlotte," she whispered in a soothing tone. "I won't leave your side until the end. You may not believe this, but I didn't want this to happen. I really didn't, but you just couldn't shut up. I can't let anyone interfere with my plans."

It only took a few minutes before Charlotte stopped breathing.

Jessica laid her down gently on the sofa. She was glad that Leah was with her grandmother so that she would not have to witness this tragedy.

She didn't enjoy taking Charlotte from her child, but the woman would not shut up. If she had just kept quiet about Jessica's affair with Mike—she would still be alive.

❦

Jessica woke up with Charlotte still heavy on her mind. She wondered how Leah was doing and decided to see for herself.

After breakfast with Clayton, she announced, "I'm going out for a few hours this morning. I need to update my wardrobe."

"Where are you really going?"

Jessica smiled. "I'm really going shopping, Clayton."

"Charlotte's mother owns a boutique," he stated. "I know all of your secrets, remember?"

She looked over at him. "I just want to make sure that the little girl is doing okay—I do care that she's growing up without her parents, although I may have done her a favor." Jessica knew that Clayton wasn't thrilled with her decision to get rid of Charlotte. He believed her death was an unnecessary one.

"Meet me back here at noon. I'll have lunch ready and then we'll go shopping for a car."

"Are we good?"

Clayton met her gaze. "Yeah. We good."

Jessica kissed him. "I know that you're only trying to keep me safe. I appreciate it, but I'm not as reckless as I was in the past. I know what I'm doing."

"And I know once your mind is made up—nothing will change it. Just be careful, babe."

"Always."

He handed her a set of keys. "Take my car. I don't plan to go anywhere until you get back."

Clayton was dressed in a pair of sweats.

"Working out this morning?" she asked.

He finished off his orange juice. "Yeah."

Jessica pushed away from the table, rose to her feet, and took their empty plates to the kitchen.

"I'll put them in the dishwasher," Clayton said.

"Honey, I got this." He had cooked so she wanted to take care of the cleaning—it was the least she could do for the man who always had her back. Clayton was always available to her whenever she needed him. He was the one constant in her life.

Clayton rose to his feet and pulled cash out of his wallet. "Here's two thousand dollars."

Jessica smiled. "Thanks."

She pulled out of the garage twenty minutes later.

Jessica waved at Nikko, who was heading toward the house. He looked like he was ready to work out as well.

Clayton's Mercedes was nice, but she already knew what she wanted. Jessica wanted a Jaguar. It was her dream car.

She parked the car in front of a boutique and got out.

Jessica wanted to check on Charlotte's daughter, Leah who was being raised by her grandmother. Marsha Adams owned the high-end shop named after her daughter. She walked inside and immediately selected a dress from the rack, holding it up to her as she eyed her reflection in a full-length mirror.

"That color really compliments your complexion."

She turned to acknowledge the stylish-dressed woman standing nearby. "It's very nice."

"I don't think I've ever seen you in the shop before." She extended her hand. "I'm Marsha."

Shaking her hand, Jessica introduced herself. "This is my first time. My fiancé and I just moved here from New York."

Charlotte had inherited her round face and facial features from her mother. Marsha looked as if she could've been Charlotte's sister. Her perfectly styled hair was cut into a cute bob with no signs of gray. Her makeup was lightly applied and enhanced her flawless complexion. Jessica's eyes traveled to a little girl seated behind the counter. "Who's the little angel over there?"

"That's my granddaughter. She's here with me most

mornings, then she goes to preschool."

"She's beautiful."

"You have children?"

Unsettled by her question, Jessica turned her attention back to her reflection. "I had a son, but he died."

"Oh honey… I'm so sorry."

Jessica picked up a black shirt. "Some things you never get over."

"You're so right about that. I still miss my daughter so much. Leah is a joy and she helps to ease the pain some."

"I'm sorry for your loss."

"Thank you, sweetie."

She held up the shirt and the dress. "I'm going to get both."

"Would you like to try them on?"

Jessica shook her head. "They'll fit fine. I'm going to look around a little more."

The doors opened.

"Natalia," Martha greeted. "How was London?"

Jessica snapped to attention. She couldn't believe her good fortune.

"Dean and I had a wonderful time. To be honest, I considered not coming back—I loved it so much."

"Well, I'm glad you decided to come home. Leah and I would've missed you terribly."

"How's my little sweetie doing?" Natalia asked.

"She misses her mom and dad. We all do."

Martha and Natalie walked up to the counter.

Her lips puckered in annoyance, Jessica watched as her nemesis picked up the little girl and planted a kiss on her chubby cheek.

"I brought you something special from London," she

was saying.

Leah's eyes grew large with delight. "Auntie Nae, what is it?"

"What do you like to play with most in the world?"

"Dolls. Did you bring me a doll?"

"I sure did," Natalia said with a short laugh. She pulled a wrapped gift from her shopping bag. "Here you go, sweetie."

The little girl kissed Natalia. "Thank you, Auntie Nae."

Jessica pretended to be interested in a red dress hanging nearby on the rack. Out of the corner of her eye, she caught Martha looking in her direction.

"Did you find something else?" she asked.

Jessica cleared her throat. "Not yet," she replied with a soft chuckle.

Natalia looked over at her, their gazes connecting.

Jessica didn't lower her eyes. She wanted to see if Natalia recognized her, despite all of the cosmetic work she'd had done.

A tiny smile formed on Jessica's lips when she looked away. Although Natalia tried not to be obvious, Jessica knew that she was still watching her. Her presence seemed to unnerve the woman who she held responsible for keeping her family out of her grasp.

She grabbed a purple sweater and carried it up to the counter. "You have such lovely pieces in here. I think I'm going to quit now."

Jessica could feel Natalia's eyes on her.

"Why don't we go to grandmama's office and open your gift. You don't mind, Martha, do you?"

"No, go right ahead," Martha responded.

"Is that another daughter?" Jessica inquired, although

she already knew the answer.

"She's my spiritual daughter. She and my daughter were close friends—like sisters really."

Lowering her voice, she added, "My only child was murdered last year."

"How terrible for you," Jessica murmured.

"She had her life stolen from her… I just hope that the person responsible is caught soon. I want to be around long enough to raise my grandbaby and see justice done for my daughter."

Jessica felt a chill snake down her spine. "I'm… I'm going to put this on my American Express."

Martha nodded. "I hope you'll come back. We are having a sale next weekend."

"I love a good sale," she responded with a smile.

"Would you like to sign up for our mailing list?"

"Sure."

Jessica walked out of the boutique with her purchases, humming softly. She hadn't expected to see Natalia so soon, but it was perfect timing.

She looked all happy and giddy, but it wasn't going to last much longer. Jessica was going to wipe that look of newlywed bliss right off Natalia's face.

※

"You're late," Clayton said. "Did you forget about our lunch date?" He took down two highball glasses from a cupboard, then opened the refrigerator door.

Jessica kissed him before plopping down onto a barstool. From her vantage, she could see everything Clayton was doing as well as the gun still poking up from the back of his slacks. "I stayed longer than I planned in the boutique. Natalia showed up."

"I hope you didn't blow your cover."

"I didn't say anything to her this time, but don't worry. We'll run into each other again."

"What would you like to drink?"

"Watermelon vodka over Sprite."

She watched him fish out the vodka.

"Just because you changed your looks doesn't mean that you won't get caught," Clayton said. "You can't let your emotions take over, Jess. That's when you make mistakes."

She eyed him. "I'm smarter than that, Clayton."

"No you're not," he responded, deftly pouring the ingredients into one of the highball glasses. "If you were— you would just enjoy your new life and forget all about the past. We have each other. Isn't that enough?" Clayton poured himself a glass of wine.

She murmured her thanks when he delivered the glass to the counter top. "I've never known you to let someone who wronged you just get away with it. After your uncle molested me, you—"

Clayton interrupted her by interjecting, "I was protecting you. You want revenge. That's different." He reached over, covering her hand with his own. "The person responsible for your pain is dead."

"I'm going to stick to our plan," she assured him. "As long as nobody interferes."

He removed a package of meat from the fridge.

"What are we having for lunch?" Jessica asked.

"Chicken fajitas."

"Want some help?"

"I got this," Clayton responded.

"I love watching you cook. You make it look very artistic."

He smiled. "A lifetime ago I dreamed of being a chef."

"You own a high-end restaurant, so part of your dream came true." Jessica took a sip of her drink.

"I actually prepared some meals for customers a few times, but mostly I work with the chef to create the menu." Clayton sautéed the onions, stirring every couple of minutes.

"Great cook, bartender… you're handsome and sexy. Why did we split up?" she asked.

"You wanted to find your mother. That desire went deeper than the desire you had for me, Jess. I know you felt I didn't support you, but I was trying to protect you—I told you that there was a chance she would reject you."

"And you were right." It pained her to admit that fact, but there was no denying the truth.

A look of tenderness passed over his features. "You have no idea how much I wanted to be wrong about this."

"I hope that you won't hold that against me."

He looked at her then. "Babe, I can never stay angry with you for long. There are times when I hated myself because of it."

"I'm not leaving you again. This time everything is going to be perfect."

Chapter 5

Natalia joined Martha at the counter. "Do you know the woman that just left here?"

"No, this is the first time she's been in the store. She mentioned that she recently moved to Raleigh from New York. I have to say that she has the most beautiful green eyes I've seen. Lovely girl…"

It was something about the woman that struck a familiar chord with Natalia. It was her walk—the way she moved her hips… it reminded her of Reina.

She did not want to say anything to Martha out of fear of upsetting her. Besides, Natalia decided she was just being paranoid. Although the woman's complexion and stride reminded her of Reina—her features were not the same whatsoever.

Natalia glanced down at the information written down for the mailing list.

"Jessica Campana."

"Campana," Martha repeated. "She's part Latina? Well, whatever she is—from the looks of it, she's got some money. She lives on Ramblewood Drive near North Hills."

Natalia nodded in agreement. "They have some beautiful homes in that area. Dean and I looked at one, but he thought it was out of our budget. Besides, he really wants us to consider Cary since it's closer to his office."

"I wonder what she does for a living," Martha said. "Did you see the way she just pulled all those hundred dollar bills out of her purse. She doesn't look like a call girl or a stripper."

Natalia agreed. "I'm sure you'll have time to get to know her. With all of the beautiful stuff you have in here— she'll be back."

"It's almost time for Leah to go to school." Martha checked her watch. "Helen should have been here by now."

"I can drop her off," Natalia said. "I don't mind and it's on the way to my house."

"Are you sure?"

She smiled. "It's fine."

Martha embraced her. "Thank you, sweetie."

Natalia dropped off Leah as promised, and then headed home.

Natalia placed her purse on the coffee table before slipping out of her shoes.

She sank down on the sofa.

She loved being married to Dean. There was a time in her life that she felt her heart belonged to Holt Deveraux. How wrong she had been. Every fiber of her being knew that Dean was the only man for her. Natalia never thought she could be this happy.

The telephone rang.

The picture of her cousin's face, prompted her to answer. "Sabrina, I'm so glad you called."

"How's married life?"

"It is absolutely wonderful," Natalia gushed. "I love every minute of it."

"So how was London?"

There was something in her voice that gave Natalia pause. "I know you didn't call me just to hear about marriage and London. What's going on?"

"You know I started a new job last month. Well, one of the executives is a former *customer* of mine. He's been trying to get me to sleep with him."

"Have you talked to H.R.?"

"No, because I don't really want to start any problems."

"You need to record everything so that you have evidence," Natalia advised. "If you want, I'll go to the office and speak with HR and the CEO as your attorney."

"Maybe I should just quit. I don't believe God would place me in this type of situation," Sabrina said. "Because if I don't do what he wants—he's going to tell everyone I used to be a prostitute."

"I wouldn't walk away without a fight, Sabrina. Start keeping notes and we'll deal with that pervert."

"Thank you."

"Record those conversations."

"I will."

Natalia hung up the phone. She picked up the photo of her father and said, "You have no idea how much Sabrina and I wish you were here. Daddy, you always had a way of making everything right."

After placing the picture frame back on the table,

Natalia settled back against the sofa cushion, clutching a throw pillow. She thought about the woman that had been in the boutique earlier. It was strange that despite obvious differences, she reminded her of Reina. It didn't make any sense. "I want this woman out of my head," she whispered to the empty room. *I'm starting to see her in innocent strangers.*

Natalia decided if she stayed busy, there was no time to think about the woman who tried to kill her. She spent the rest of her day arranging furniture and putting away clothes.

An hour before Dean was due home, she started dinner.

"Honey, I'm home."

At the sound of his voice, she glanced at the clock. Dean was home early.

"I'm in the kitchen," Natalia said. "Sweetheart, how was your day?"

"It was good." He walked up to her and planted a kiss on her lips. "But I missed you like crazy."

"Dean, are you sure about going into ministry full-time?"

He nodded. "It's what I was called to do, but are you still okay with it?"

"Of course," Natalia responded. "I think I want to get back into the courtroom. I like your suggestion about starting my own firm. I can work from home for now. If I need to meet with a client, I can rent an office from the company down the street."

"Getting back to work will do you some good," Dean said.

She agreed.

Thirty minutes later, they sat down at the table to eat dinner.

"Everything looks delicious, baby."

Proud of the fact that she hadn't burned their meal, Natalia smiled. "Thanks." She considered taking cooking lessons since it was a skill she had not yet perfected.

"How is Martha?"

"She's fine," Natalia said. "She is slowly getting back to her old self. Oh, while I was at the boutique, I saw this woman earlier… Dean, there was something about her that reminded me of

Reina." She shook her head. "It definitely wasn't her, but I'm beginning to feel like I can't get her out of my head."

"Hon, maybe it's time you talked to someone. You're anxious and scared all the time.

You—"

Natalia interrupted Dean by interjecting, "I don't need a therapist. What I need is that psycho behind bars somewhere." She stuck a forkful of salad into her mouth.

He wiped his mouth on the edge of his napkin. "You went through something very traumatic. It might help."

"I'm fine."

Her husband didn't push the subject and she was grateful.

They finished dinner and cleaned the kitchen together.

Later, while Dean was in his home office on a call, Natalia's mind traveled back to her last encounter with Reina.

"…Jessie Belle rejected you, which made you angry and then you pushed her over that balcony."

"Interesting theory, but no evidence…" Her eyes. Reina's eyes told a story of their own. Although she appeared cordial, her eyes exposed a hidden evil underneath, that scared Natalia.

"I don't need an admission from you." She told Reina. "I just want you to stop pointing that gun at me and leave my house. If you do that, I'll see that you get your journal back."

Reina regarded her quizzically for a moment. "What journal?"

Natalia did not respond. She had foolishly said too much.

She thought about the journal she had taken from Reina's house. Looking back, she probably never should've mentioned it, but Natalia had been scared out of her mind. She believed that's what set Reina off that day.

"I want my journal back."

"That's not going to happen," Natalia stated. "As long as you keep pointing that gun at me."

Natalia shook away the troubling thoughts. She never wanted to think about Reina, but the witch kept creeping to the forefront of her mind. It was time for her to get back to work so she could focus her energies on something more productive.

She did not want to give thought to the past or the woman who sought to try and end her life. Reina was gone and it was time that she be forgotten.

Chapter 6

Jessica ran into Natalia the following week at Crabtree Mall. She followed her into *Kanki*, a Japanese steak house.

"One please," she told the hostess.

Seated in the waiting area, Natalia glanced up.

Jessica gave her a polite smile, then turned her attention back to the waitress.

"If you're dining alone, we could share a table," Natalia offered. "I hate eating alone."

"So do I," Jessica said after a moment. *This is going to be easier than I thought.*

She held out a hand. "I'm Natalia Anderson. I saw you at Charlotte's. Martha, the owner is like a mother to me."

"That's right. You were there talking to the little girl. My name is Jessica. Jessica Campana."

Natalia smiled. "Martha mentioned that you were new in town."

"Guilty," Jessica murmured. "I've been here for about a month now."

"Did you transfer because of a job?"

"In a way," she responded. "My fiancé has business dealings here, so this is going to be home for a while." Jessica grudgingly admired the chic black and white pantsuit Natalia was wearing. Her decision to pair it with red jewelry, handbag and shoes was a good one.

"Jessica, congratulations on your engagement." Hand to her chest, Natalia gushed, "I'm a newlywed myself. I got married a couple of weeks ago."

"You're certainly glowing." She resisted the urge to whip out a knife and cut Natalia's throat. Red was all she saw when it came to her. *I promised Clayton that I would do things his way this time.*

They were led to a bar area bistro table.

Jessica bit back a smile over the way Natalia was fawning over her, a huge contrast to the way she was treated when the witch thought she was just a hairstylist.

"Thanks so much for allowing me to join you for lunch."

"Natalia, it's not a problem," Jessica said smoothly. I appreciate the company. Clayton was supposed to join me, but had a conflict at the last moment."

"Clayton. Is that your fiancé?"

"Yes." *Wow, you sure are nosy, aren't you?*

Natalia chattered on. "Have you been here before?"

"No," Jessica lied. "Clayton told me about it and so I thought I'd give it a try. He knows how much I love Asian cuisine."

"This is one of my favorite restaurants," Natalia said. "You'll love it."

Jessica glanced around. "Looks like we're missing the show." A few feet from them, groups were seated together surrounding teppanyaki grills watching as chefs chopped, diced and cooked with the flip of a knife and a spatula.

"I only like to sit and watch them cook the food when I'm with friends."

She had no idea that Natalia was such a chatterbox. Jessica pretended to study the menu, although she already knew what she wanted. She loved the hibachi shrimp. She looked up to find Natalia gazing at her.

"I apologize if I keep staring," she said. "It's just that you have certain mannerisms that remind me of someone."

"From the expression on your face…I'm not sure it's not a good thing."

"Not really, but I won't bore you with the details," Natalia stated. "You're not her and that's a wonderful thing. *Trust me.*"

Jessica smiled. "On that note, I'm glad I'm not that person."

"I'm super thrilled."

After they placed their orders, Natalia said, "I would love to have you and your fiancé over for dinner. Who knows… maybe this will be the start of a new friendship."

"That's really sweet of you."

"If you're looking for a wedding planner, the one I used was absolutely fabulous. She did a fantastic job."

Jessica smiled. "I will definitely need her information."

They spent two hours talking over lunch.

"It was nice running into you," Jessica said as they walked out of the restaurant.

"You didn't have to pay for my lunch, but thank you."

She handed her ticket to the valet. "Like you said,

this may be the beginning of a new friendship."

❧

"Babe, you are not going to believe this… we're having dinner with Natalia and her husband on Friday." When she arrived home, Jessica found Clayton in the kitchen preparing salmon for dinner.

Without looking up, he said, "You certainly work fast."

"She actually approached me. We had lunch together at *Kanki*." Jessica washed her hands, and then sliced a lemon. "How about steamed broccoli to go with the salmon?"

Clayton nodded. "I placed a couple of potatoes in the oven already."

Jessica retrieved a plastic container from the refrigerator. "By the way, I told her that I had a fiancé." She opened the container, dropping the broccoli into the food steamer.

"Well, I guess we'd better go ring shopping." Clayton said with a chuckle. "Unless you trust me to pick out something for you."

"You don't have to buy me a ring."

"If you want her to believe your story—you need an engagement ring."

Jessica embraced him. "You are so good to me."

"Just so you know, this ring …"

"Clayton, don't worry… I'll give it back to you when I'm done."

"Actually, I was *going* to say that you can keep it if you agree to be my wife. Jess, I'm ready to settle down. You are the woman I love and I want to marry you."

"Baby, I want you to know that if I ever decide to get

married—it will be to you. I'm kind of a mess right now and you deserve so much better."

"We've been through a lot together. *I know you.*"

Jessica hated talking about marriage because it always seemed to lead to an argument. Things were good between her and Clayton—she wanted to keep it that way. "Why don't we change the subject for now?"

"Maybe you should've said you lived with your brother." Clayton opened the oven to check on the salmon.

She placed a hand to his cheek. "That would never work. The way I look at you would give me away. You're much too sexy to be my brother."

He laughed. "Whatever."

Jessica washed her hands, then turned her attention back to cooking. "Will Nikko and Miguel be joining us for dinner?"

"Yeah, unless you just want it to be the two of us."

She checked on the potatoes. "It's fine. I really like them."

Her lips curved. Everything was working per her plan. This time there would be no mistakes.

Chapter 7

Chrissy decided to have Holt come to her house for their first meeting. It was a comfortable place for her since it was her home. Feeling a bit anxious, she took her medication and tried to relax.

Holt arrived shortly after two.

She opened the door and stepped aside to let him enter.

"You look like Mom," he stated.

Chrissy was not sure how to respond. Her stomach was still clenched tight.

"I'm glad you agreed to meet me."

She gestured for him to sit down. "Holt, I never wanted to interfere in your life. I confronted Jessie Belle only because I wanted to know why she didn't keep me."

"You're not interfering, Chrissy. You're my sister."

Chrissy sat down in one of the accent chairs. "Have you heard from Reina?"

He shook his head. "I don't really expect to—she's done a lot of bad things, but she is still our sister, so I pray for her."

"I'm still trying to wrap my head around that," Chrissy confessed. "I can't believe that she and I are twins."

"It's time you met the rest of the family," Holt stated with a smile. "There's my wife, Frankie. And you have a nephew and twin nieces."

"I heard," she murmured. "Traynor called me when the babies were born."

"I never thought being a father would make me this happy."

"I used to think that I didn't want children, but now..." Chrissy paused a moment before continuing. "I'd like to have a son or a daughter."

"It's not too late," Holt said.

"I'm thirty-four... not exactly a spring chicken. I don't even have a husband." She broke into a smile. "I'll just have to spoil your children."

"So you don't have anyone special in your life?"

She thought about Aiden. He called her a couple of times, but she had yet to accept his invitation for dinner. Her resolve was weakening, although Chrissy would never admit it aloud. "No, I'm very single."

"Is this by choice?" Holt inquired.

Chrissy nodded. "I'm focusing on me right now."

"Do you have any questions about mom?"

She eyed him. "Not really. I think I know enough about her."

"There were parts of her that was good, Chrissy," Holt said. "She used to be the loudest person at my games cheering for me. Back then, I was so embarrassed... Mom could sing. Did you know this?"

"Really?" She hadn't heard about her possessing any

type of musical talent. "Did she play any instruments?"

"She played piano."

"I heard that you sing as well."

Holt nodded. "What about you?"

"Not my gift," she responded with a grin. "Did you ever sing with Jessie Belle?" Chrissy wasn't sure why she posed the question, but she was interested in hearing about his relationship with their mother.

"Yeah, we did a few times. I didn't like it though. It wasn't cool to sing with your mom."

"It was probably pretty corny."

Chrissy loved the sound of her brother's laughter.

"I want to know more about your life, but we don't have to do it this time around."

"I grew up in group homes until I decided to become a prostitute to escape that life," she said. "I gave it up and last year, I was introduced to Jesus. My life changed after that and now, I'm a partner of a real estate business." There wasn't any point in delaying the truth. Holt would either accept or reject her.

"Won't He do it…"

She smiled and nodded.

Holt rose to his feet and walked over to where she was sitting.

Taking her hands in his, he helped her stand.

"Chrissy, I want you to know that I am honored to have you as my sister. I'm sure there is much that we can learn from one another. I would like the opportunity to do so as brother and sister."

She swallowed her tears. "This is all I've ever wanted, Holt."

He wiped away a tear on her face. "Won't He do it…"

Chrissy embraced her brother. "I am very proud to be your sister."

They spent the next two hours looking at the photo album he brought with him and talking. This time spent with Holt was a dream come true for Chrissy.

Chapter 8

Mary Ellen wiped her mouth on the edge of her napkin. "I've noticed that you hardly ever mention her anymore."

Traynor looked up from his plate. "There's no reason to mention somebody I never really knew. Our marriage started out and ended with a lie."

"Jessie Belle is gone. There is no need to hold onto anger."

He shrugged. "I'm having a hard time forgiving her, Mary Ellen." Traynor's eyes roamed around the restaurant in Briar Creek where he and Mary Ellen had dinner once a week.

"I know you feel betrayed."

"I'm trying to get past all I've learned about her, but it's hard. When I think of those girls and how they suffered—I hate what they had to deal with growing up."

"Jessie Belle was young, Traynor. And under the influence of her mother. The deception was encouraged by her mother who believed that a good man would not want her daughter because she wasn't a virgin." Mary Ellen eyed Traynor. "Looking back, do you think that you would've married Jessie Belle if you'd known the truth about her?"

He wiped his mouth on the corner of his napkin. "Probably not, but then again, I might have—I don't like the fact that I wasn't given a choice in the matter."

"Despite everything, Jessie Belle loved you."

"Not enough to trust me with the truth," he said. "I'm speaking at Mayville Baptist Church on Sunday. I'm trying to decide if I'm going to visit the gravesite while I'm in Georgia." Traynor finished off his iced tea.

"It might do you good."

Traynor shrugged. "I don't know."

"Why don't you just wait until you're down there to decide?"

"I will." He pushed his plate away. "I don't know about you, but I'm full. I think I'm going to pass on dessert this time."

"I'm getting mine to go. I'll eat it later."

Traynor looked at Mary Ellen. "Why haven't you married again?"

She shrugged. "I didn't make a conscious decision not to marry. I guess I'm so busy with church and work obligations… I don't think about having anyone in my life. I'm good." Mary Ellen shifted in her chair. "What about you? Do you think you'll ever get married again?"

"I don't know. It's hard to say right now. When it happens—I'm going to be much wiser this time around."

Chapter 9

Seated in the booth behind Mary Ellen and Traynor, Jessica could hear most of their conversation. She donned a blond wig and dark sunglasses as a disguise. She wasn't ready to reveal her new look to them. Jessica had gone by the church earlier and followed Traynor to the restaurant. It only took a crisp twenty-dollar bill to get the hostess to seat her behind them.

"How are things going with your search for an assistant?" Traynor asked.

"I'm still looking for one. The ones I've interviewed—none of them were right for me."

Jessica smiled, then made a mental note to apply for the position as soon as she was back home. This was not a part of her plan, but she could work with it. As Mary Ellen's assistant, she could insert herself into the lives of the Deveraux family.

She finished off the last of her cheese fries. This was

going to be so perfect. Jessica couldn't wait to share the news with Clayton.

Traynor and Mary Ellen prepared to leave.

Jessica took a minute to look at Mary Ellen Reed. Everything about her was perfect—hair, makeup and clothes. She was relieved to hear that she had no interest in Traynor outside of friendship. But it bothered Jessica that Mary Ellen remained so loyal to her wretched mother.

She exited the restaurant ten minutes after them.

During the ride home, Jessica recalled the day that she revealed the truth of her birth to Jessie Belle. It was ingrained in her memory so that she would never forget it.

"The reason I wanted to see you is because there's something you need to know."

"What is so important that I needed to meet you here?"

"Your mother lied to you," Jessie said. *"Anabeth knew that your daughter survived that night."*

It took Jessie Belle a moment to recover from the shock of her words. *"What in the world are you talking about? I don't have a daughter."*

"Yes, you do. Gloria Ricks told me how you cried that night; how you begged your mother to let you see the child."

"I don't know any Gloria Ricks."

"Jessie Belle, you don't have to worry. I'm not here to blackmail you—it's nothing like that."

"Then what are you after?"

"It's time you learned the truth about that night."

She folded her arms across her chest. *"I'm listening."*

"Your mother was upset because you hid your pregnancy until it was too late for you to have an abortion. As soon as she discovered it, she brought you to Gloria. Labor had to be induced…"

"Go on," Jessie Belle said, "It's getting interesting."

"You had a little girl that night, only you were a bit delirious from the pain and exhaustion. Anabeth told you the baby was stillborn. You wanted to see the infant, but they wouldn't let you."

"Considering whether there's any truth to this little story of yours—what happened to the child?"

"Gloria took the baby home and raised her."

"I heard that Gloria died in a fire."

"She did," Jessica confirmed. "I was fourteen when it happened."

Jessie Belle shook her head. "See, I was told that she had a daughter, and that girl was pregnant."

"That girl was me. It's true that I gave birth to a son and he was stillborn—I know because I held my child in my arms and saw for myself. Gloria wasn't my birth mother—I am the daughter you thought died that night."

"It was cruel of your mother to tell you such lies."

"Did you hear me? I said you are my mother, Jessie Belle. Gloria told me."

"This is absurd."

"They were not good people. Henry Ricks molested me and he was the father of my child."

Jessie Belle looked shocked. "I'm sorry that you had to go through something like this."

"I don't blame you for anything that happened. They stole your daughter."

"I need you to listen to me," Jessie Belle began. "I am not your mother. Gloria told you a bunch of lies."

"At least you're not denying that you know her any longer."

"What is it that you really want from me?" she asked.

"I want you in my life. We were torn apart, but we can

fix that now."

Jessie Belle burst into a harsh laugh. *"You've got to be kidding me?"*

"I am willing to take a DNA test to prove my claim."

"You're not the only person who has come pretending to be related to me." She paused a moment before adding, *"Gloria apparently told that lie to another girl as well. She came to me looking for money and a so-called DNA test. It was proven that I wasn't her mother. As you said, Gloria wasn't a nice person and if she hadn't died—she would have most likely contacted me by now in some attempt to extort money."*

"Why would you say that?" Jessica asked.

"Because that was the kind of person she was," she responded.

Jessica eyed her, studying her expression. *"You knew..."*

"The only thing I knew was that she used to threaten to expose my secrets if my mother didn't give her money."

"But you had to know that I was alive."

"Not really. I lived in a small town and my father was a well-respected pastor. My mother was determined that my sins would not come to tarnish his reputation."

"How could you so easily turn your back on the child you claimed to want?"

"My mother was right. I was too young to be a parent."

"And now?"

"You were misinformed, but even if it were true—my husband and son would never understand."

"Gloria wouldn't have lied to me about this."

"She allowed her husband to live after molesting you. A woman who will stay with a man that vile—she's capable of anything. I bet she tried to blame you."

Jessica didn't respond.

"I knew it."

"I am your daughter, Jessie Belle."

"There is nothing I can do for you. It's best that you go on with your life and never mention this again." Jessie Belle rose to her feet. "I can be an advocate for you or your enemy, but I can never be your mother. I hope that we understand one another."

"I understand that you're one selfish b—" Jessica shook her head. "I was in awe of you when I first saw you, but after hearing about how you screw over people … I'm lucky that I wasn't raised by the infamous Jessie Belle Deveraux. You are no better than your mother—selfish and manipulative."

"Not another word about my mom," she warned. "And whatever you think of me … I have no problem owning it."

"Would you like a refill on your iced tea?" her waitress asked, propelling Jessica back to the present.

"No, thank you. I'm getting ready to leave."

Jessica stood up and pushed her sunglasses up as she strolled toward the exit door.

⁂

"Do you think it's wise to be so close to Mary Ellen?" Clayton asked.

"This gives me an opportunity to be near my brother and step-father. You know that saying: keep your friends close and your enemies closer." Jessica clicked the send button on the screen. "It's done. I've applied for the position."

"Honey, we've talked about triggers—there are some things that just send you into a rage.

When you get like that—mistakes are made."

She released a soft sigh. "Clayton, I'm fine."

"Do you really think you can spend time with two women you hate?"

Jessica placed the laptop on the coffee table. "Honey, I know the end game. I can do this."

"That pastor tried to control you and look what happened. You *killed* him."

Jessica stiffened. "How long are you going to keep throwing that in my face?"

Clayton took a seat beside her. "I'm just reminding you how easily things can spin of control for you when you are enraged."

"I kept my control where Jessie Belle was concerned."

He gave her a sidelong glance. "Did you?"

"I didn't push her over that balcony, Clayton. She was my mother." She leaned back against the cushions on the sofa. "Maybe that's why God took my son. Anabeth, Jessie Belle and even me—none of us should have been mothers. We're bad seeds."

"Babe, you would've been a great mother."

"Sometimes, I wonder if Gloria did something to me so that the baby wouldn't survive."

"It doesn't do any good to think that way."

"We tried to have a child together, but I kept miscarrying. It's pretty clear to me that God doesn't want me to be a mom."

Clayton wrapped an arm around her. "We have each other."

He was right, but Jessica refused to settle for that. She wanted more and she was determined to get everything she wanted.

❧

Jessica ran her fingers through her hair as she eyed her reflection in the mirror. "How do I look?" She had chosen to wear a purple and white color block dress to Natalia's house for dinner.

"Beautiful," Clayton responded. "Now c'mon. We don't want to be late."

She glanced over her shoulder at him. "Why are you in such a rush?"

"I thought you wanted to make a good impression on these people. The last thing I want to do is dinner with a preacher and a woman you hate. I can't even drink like I want."

She laughed. "Who knows… you might just find Jesus after all these years."

"I doubt that," Clayton said. "Half of the people in church every Sunday can't find Jesus."

"When you hear Traynor preach, you'll feel different. He's the real deal when it comes to being a pastor."

"I know a few ministers, Jess. They are some of my best customers."

"They are not all bad."

"And they are not all good, either. Case in point, Michael Jennings. He had an affair with you and he embezzled money from the church."

Jessica kissed him. "Let's go."

"Nice house," Clayton said as he pulled into the driveway twenty minutes later.

"Ours is bigger and better." Jessica broke into a grin as she wiggled her fingers on her left hand. "So is my engagement ring."

"I bought that ring because I am serious about marrying you."

"I know. I love you, Clayton as much as I know how to love."

He reached over and gave her hand a gentle squeeze. "I'm going to take care of you, Jess."

"First, I need Natalia taken care of," she responded. Once she was no longer a threat to her, Jessica could consider a marriage to Clayton.

"Things will be set in motion after tonight."

"Just knowing that she is going to jail is the only thing that makes this dinner bearable for me. It's too bad we didn't think of this before I went through the trouble of changing my looks."

"I told you not to do it in the first place. You have never been patient, Jess. If you'd just let me take care of this in the first place."

She sighed. "Let's not start this again, Clayton."

"I'm just saying…"

She kissed him. "I guess we should make our way to the door."

Clayton got out, then walked around the car to open the door for Jessica.

She stepped out. "Grab the gift basket please."

Natalia answered the door immediately. "Welcome to our home."

She was soon joined by her husband.

Jessica held out the gift basket to Natalia. "We bought this for you."

"This is terribly sweet of you."

"You mentioned that you are newlyweds so we thought the two of you might enjoy a nice glass of Champagne and chocolate covered strawberries. Just add some candles and you have the makings for an evening of romance."

Natalia hugged her. "Thank you."

Jessica glanced over at Clayton. Recognizing the amused glint in his gaze, she sent a sharp glare in his direction.

After introductions were made, they sat down in the living room.

Natalia brought out a tray of mini crab cakes for them to nibble on.

"You have a beautiful home," Jessica said, after a subtle prompting from Clayton. "I noticed that you have a 'for sale' sign in the yard." Dean and Natalia's house wasn't as large as theirs, but it was a nice size and the furnishings contemporary. Hardwoods seemed to flow throughout the house, including the guest bedroom that was on the main floor.

"We're looking for a place in Cary so that we're closer to Dean's job."

Good luck with that, Jessica thought to herself. The only place Natalia would be moving is to a prison.

"So how did you two meet?" Natalia asked as they dined on chicken Marsala.

Jessica glanced over at Clayton, who said, "We've known each other since we were children. I lived two blocks away from her. But it wasn't until she was fourteen that we finally connected.

We've been together off and on since then."

"I wasn't ready to commit until last year," Jessica interjected, "but I've always known that he was my soulmate."

"How romantic," Natalia gushed. "I have to say; I love being married. We met a little over a year ago, but it didn't take me long to figure out that he was the only man for me."

"Where is your bathroom?" Clayton inquired after dinner.

"It's right over there," Dean told him.

He excused himself.

"Thank you again for inviting us over," Jessica said. "The meal was delicious and we enjoyed spending time with you and Dean."

Natalia reached over and gave her husband a light squeeze. "I'm glad you and Clayton were able to come."

Dean agreed. "It's nice meeting other happy couples."

"Well, we'd like to return the offer. Clayton and I both love to cook."

"Sounds like we're in for a treat," Natalia responded.

Jessica smiled. "That and more."

"I don't know about you, but I'm in need of a mani/pedi. Would you like to join me tomorrow at noon?" asked Natalia. "That's if you're not busy."

"It's a date," she responded. "Text me the name and address of the shop and I'll meet you there."

"They seem like nice people," Clayton said when they were on the way home.

"She's irritating," Jessica uttered. "I don't know how Dean puts up with her. Did you see the way she just hangs all over him? She's so pathetic."

"Different strokes for different folks."

Jessica chuckled. "Your mom used to say that."

"She was right, too."

"Did you take care of it?" she asked.

"Yeah. All of the evidence is stashed away in the toilet bowl of their guest bathroom."

"Perfect." She pressed her lips in satisfaction.

As soon as they arrived home, Jessica said, "I'm going to change into something sexy."

"While you doing that, I need to holla at my boys."

She kissed him. "Don't make me wait too long."

Jessica mood was cheerful. Things were going according to plan. Now all she had to do was sit back and wait.

Chapter 10

"I really like Jessica," Natalia said as she readied for bed. "Clayton was quiet, but he seemed nice."

"They're a nice couple."

She glanced over at her husband. "That's all you have to say about them?"

"I got the impression that Clayton was uneasy being here with us."

Natalia seemed surprised by his words. "Really?"

"He didn't look comfortable," Dean answered as he slipped out of his shirt. "I could be wrong about this, because I don't really know anything about the man. I'm not saying it's a red flag or anything. Clayton may not like being around people."

"Didn't you invite him to play golf?"

"I did, but he said it wasn't his game."

"Well, maybe it will take some time for the two of you to bond." Natalia picked up a throw pillow and sat it in a nearby accent chair."

"Honey, it's fine for you and Jessica to hang out. Not everyone is comfortable being around a minister."

"I love your company." She gave him a seductive wink. "I'm feeling like I could use some company tonight in this king-sized bed."

"I'm more than happy to join you." He walked up to her.

Natalia smiled as her husband pulled her into his arms. "I hope you were serious about starting a family right away."

"I am."

"Good because I'm ovulating."

A look of tenderness passed over his features. "I love you."

"I never tire of hearing you say that."

She closed her eyes, sending up a quick prayer. "*Thank you Father for sending me such a wonderful man. This season is the happiest I've been since losing my dad. I pray that you keep my marriage because it is sacred. Let nothing or no one succeed in tearing us apart. In Jesus Name, I pray. Amen.*"

Chapter 11

Chrissy stood up and opened the glass door. Leaving her shoes behind, she crossed the patio. The sand was cold; the ocean air was warm. There was a breeze that tousled her hair. She prowled the perimeter of the beach house. If she could, Chrissy would spend every weekend in Wilmington. She loved the small coastal town.

She twirled, arms out, her curly locks floating. There had been a time not too long ago when her pain was so intense that Chrissy thought she would die. That time was almost forgotten. She was in a good place.

She strolled down toward the ocean.

Chrissy spied a couple a few yards away, walking hand in hand. A wave of loneliness welled up in her. She was ready to share her life with someone special, but before that could happen, Chrissy knew she would have to come clean about her past. Only a man who could love her unconditionally would be able to handle the truth.

Her mind drifted to Aiden. Just thinking about him made her whole being swell with waiting. *So why do I keep turning down his invitations?* Chrissy felt an eager affection coming from him and the attraction was mutual.

She remained cautious because she didn't want to revert to her old ways. She was committed to staying on the right path—her ministry was important to her. Chrissy wanted to be sure Aiden was a man sent by God, and not a temptation designed to distract her from her calling.

Raising her eyes toward the heavens, Chrissy smiled. "Thank you for loving me, Father."

An hour later, she returned to the beach house.

During her walk, Chrissy noted there were several houses available for sale. As much time as she spent in Wilmington, maybe it was time to consider buying a home in the area. It was worth thinking about.

Her cell phone rang.

It was Aiden.

"How are you enjoying your time away?" he asked.

"I'm having a great time." Chrissy settled down on the sofa. She enjoyed their conversations. Aiden had a great sense of humor and was always in a great mood.

"Miss me?"

"Actually, I haven't given you a single thought," she said.

"Liar."

Chrissy laughed. "Okay, maybe a little."

"I thought about driving to Wilmington, but I didn't want you to think I was stalking you."

"One day we'll come up for the day."

"You won't have dinner with me, but you're willing to go to the beach?"

"That's because I can push you in the ocean."

He chuckled. "I promise you I'll be on my best behavior."

They spent the next hour on the telephone.

When Chrissy hung up, she rose to her feet and walked toward the kitchen. She'd purchased the ingredients for shrimp scampi, and prepared to cook.

There was a part of her that wished Aiden had come to Wilmington with her, but she was right to keep him at bay. Although the house she'd rented for the weekend had two bedrooms, his being here would have been too tempting.

Chrissy thought about the chocolate and peanut butter fudge on the counter. It was the only temptation she needed in her life right now.

Chapter 12

Traynor drove out to the Mayville Cemetery before heading back to Raleigh.

"I wasn't going to come here today," he said as he kneeled in front of Jessie Belle's grave. "I can't leave town without telling you how I feel."

Traynor glanced around. There were a couple of people visiting graves, most likely out of love, but not him. He was here to accuse.

"We spent thirty-one years together, but I have no real idea of who you really are, Jessie Belle. I loved you with every fiber of my being and it was never enough. You lied throughout our entire marriage." He shook his head. "I defended you to everyone. I was nothing but a fool."

He released a deep sigh. "You've left such a mess behind because of your selfishness. You knew that you had a daughter that was alive and well, but you rejected her. Jessie Belle, she was your daughter. *How could you be so cruel?*" Traynor paused a moment before saying, "There is one thing that you don't know—you have two daughters. You gave birth to twins that night."

A tear rolled down his cheek. "I don't know if I'll ever come back here to see you. Your lies have destroyed what was left of my love for you. I truly hope that you made your peace with God before you died."

Traynor left the grave and walked along the dusty path back to the car. His heart broke a little more with each step. He also felt foolish. Jessie Belle Holt was only eighteen years old when he first laid eyes on her. Traynor was so enthralled by her angelic face and those gorgeous gray eyes…members of her father's church had tried to warn him, but he refused to listen.

Perhaps if he'd taken time to court her instead of getting married just two weeks after their meeting—he might have seen the real Jessie Belle. *I loved her dearly.*

Traynor took his marriage seriously, which is why he decided to stay and work things out with his wife. Toward the end, Jessie Belle was no longer that manipulative, deceitful woman she used to be, but she still had her secrets.

The question of whether she ever truly loved him, nagged at him. Traynor kept reminding himself that Jessie Belle was gone, so it no longer mattered. However, for his male pride—he needed to know if their life together had been just one huge manipulation.

Chapter 13

Jessica walked out of the radio station with a huge grin. Her interview with Mary Ellen went so well that she was hired on the spot.

Her plan was progressing nicely. According to Clayton, the police would soon get an anonymous tip informing them that Natalia was behind the murders of Pastor Michael Jennings and his wife. He had even managed to have someone Photoshop compromising photos of the pastor and Natalia.

"You wanted me in jail, but you're going to be the one sitting behind bars."

Once she was in the car, Jessica placed a call to her nemesis. "I got the job."

"Congratulations," Natalia screamed in the phone, forcing her to remove the phone from her ear.

"What are you doing later today?"

"Nothing. What's up?"

"Why don't you come by the house? I can make us a light lunch."

"What time?"

Jessica glanced at her watch. How about one o'clock?"

"I'll see you then."

Her next phone call was to Clayton. "Hon, I invited Natalia over for lunch. I hope you don't mind."

"I'm on my way to a meeting, so we're good."

"Are Nikko and Miquel with you?"

"Yeah."

"Be careful."

"I'll give you a call when we're on our way back to the house."

Jessica knew that he could handle himself, but it didn't lessen her worry about Clayton. She wished he would rid himself of his illegal dealings and just focus on his legitimate holdings like the check cashing businesses and his restaurant. He had recently opened a check cashing business in Danville, Virginia since North Carolina wouldn't allow them.

⚡

Jessica stepped aside to let Natalia into the house.

"This house is *amazing*."

"Thank you." A smile tugged at her lips when she glimpsed a flash of envy in Natalia's eyes.

"I used to want a house like this—five thousand square feet or more, a huge kitchen like this."

"And you don't anymore?" Jessica asked.

"Not really." Natalia glanced at her. "Dean and I are trying to start a family. We are saving up for private school and college education."

"Are you pregnant?"

Natalia shook her head. "We're trying though."

If Jessica didn't hate her so much, she might have been happy for Natalia. "I made a chef's salad for lunch."

"Yummy."

Jessica rolled her eyes heavenward. The witch was getting on her nerves already. She couldn't wait to get Natalia out of her house.

They ate on the patio.

"I've never heard you mention any family," Jessica said.

"My parents are gone and the only person I'm really close to is a cousin named Sabrina. She lives here in Raleigh."

"I understand," she responded. "I'm not close to my family for the most part."

Natalia took a sip of her tea. "I had time to grieve my mother, but my dad died unexpectedly and I really miss him."

"What happened, if you don't mind my asking."

"He committed suicide, but he might as well had been murdered." Natalia sat back in her chair. "My father was gay and he was trying to deal with it privately. There was someone who wanted our church, so he was blackmailed. Rather than risk exposure, my dad decided to kill himself."

"Talk about drama in the church," Jessica uttered.

"I'm glad that the person responsible is dead," Natalia said. "Remember the woman I say you remind me of?" When Jessica nodded, she continued, "She's the daughter of the person who destroyed my father."

"Is this why you dislike her?"

"She tried to kill me—that's why I can't stand breathing the same air as her. This woman is just as evil as her mother."

Under the table, Jessica balled her hands into fists. "Where is she now?"

"Far away from me, I hope." Natalia wiped her mouth with her napkin. "I'm just glad that North Carolina is a capital punishment state. When she is finally caught—I'm going to push for lethal injection at her sentencing."

Jessica refilled Natalia's glass with lemonade. "I'm surprised with this, considering the fact that you're married to a pastor."

Natalia stared at her. "It took a long time for me to forgive her mother, but Reina ... she tried to kill me. She burned my house down with me in it."

"Apparently, it was God's will that you survive."

"I'm so thankful."

"I don't want to seem unkind, but what was your part in all this? I mean, why would this girl go through all of that trouble to hurt you?"

"I knew things about Reina that I don't believe she wanted others to know."

"Were you blackmailing her?" Jessica questioned.

Natalia gasped. "No. Of course not."

"I'm just kidding ... why don't we change the subject?"

"I'm all for that."

They exchanged a polite, simultaneous smile.

Jessica counted the minutes until she could escort Natalia to the door. She made a mental note to have Clayton move things up.

"You have a guest house?"

"Yes," Jessica responded.

"Have you and Clayton talked about having a family?"

Natalia stuck a forkful of salad into her mouth.

"We're still talking about it."

Jessica looked away, frowning with cold fury.

She half-listened as Natalia chattered while they finished eating. Maybe it was their seven-year age difference, but Jessica found her annoying. She could've shouted for joy when Natalia left an hour later.

It was almost three when Clayton returned home.

"I was getting worried," she said when he entered the kitchen.

"I needed to make a couple of stops."

"You good?"

His expressive face changed and became almost somber. "Yeah."

"Are you hungry?"

"Not really. I have to go out later so I'll grab something then." He removed his blazer. "How was lunch with your frenemy?"

"Every time she opened her mouth, I just wanted to choke her. She blames Jessie Belle for her father's suicide. I can't prove it, but I really believe she's the one who pushed my mother over that balcony."

"We nearly have everything in place."

"I can't wait to see her face when I visit her in jail. I'm sure she'll be sobbing all over the place."

"Just don't blow your cover, Jess."

"I won't," she said. "I'm going to be her friend until the day I visit her in prison. Do they allow death row inmates to have visitors?"

Clayton sank down beside her. "Don't get too ahead of yourself, babe."

"Our plan is going to work."

"There is always that chance that something can come up—we have to be realists."

Jessica turned to face him. "She will either go away to prison or Natalia has to die. There are no other alternatives."

❧

Jessica was up bright and early to prepare for her first day as Mary Ellen's assistant. She came downstairs to a breakfast prepared by Clayton.

"I wondered where you were," she said before kissing him. "I thought maybe you were out on a jog."

"I wanted to make you something to eat before you left for work."

"You made my favorite... spinach and mushroom omelet."

"I made some bacon, sausages and toast, too."

Jessica glanced around the kitchen. "Why did you cook so much food?"

"Nikko and Miquel will be here shortly."

She sat down at the table. Although she didn't say anything to Clayton, she knew that something was up with him. He was new to Raleigh, and she was sure that his competitors weren't too happy about his relocation. Jessica pretended not to notice that he'd upgraded the surveillance equipment, and had installed cameras on the gate.

She had been to the guesthouse a couple of times. A complete computer system was set up there like the one in the house. Jessica also knew about the house Clayton recently purchased near Crabtree Valley Mall.

"Can you answer a question for me?" she asked. "Why

did you buy that house? I saw the paperwork on your desk."

This house is under a corporation I own and it can't easily be linked to me. The other house is in my name."

"So if anyone is looking for you—they won't find you here."

He nodded. "Some more of my guys are moving here from New York. They will be staying in the other house."

"Is there anything I need to worry about?"

Clayton shook his head. "No."

He laid a copy of the News & Observer in front of her. The caption read: *Drug Dealer Shot and Killed in the Triangle.* "Not anymore."

Jessica took a sip of her orange juice. "Cool."

❧

The first thing Jessica noticed was the aquarium in Mary Ellen's office. "Nice reef collection."

"Thank you," she said. "I have one here and at home."

"I have a friend who has a huge tank. He's been at it for years now."

"I'm just getting started," Mary Ellen said. "A friend of mine just gave me some of his leather coral. He said it was great for beginners."

"It looks like you're doing a great job with it."

Mary Ellen smiled. "I still have a lot to learn, but I'm enjoying it."

Jessica followed her through the station where the administrative offices were located.

"This is where you'll be working. My office is in there."

"Great," she murmured.

"We are hosting a gala in two weeks. We do this annually on the night before the Sapphire Awards."

"Sapphire Awards?"

"This award was created to highlight the accomplishments of African Americans who have succeeded against immense odds."

Although she knew all about the awards, Jessica pretended otherwise. She had to keep up the pretense that she was a new resident of the city.

"Here's your invitation. I want you to enjoy yourself this time. Next year, you'll be working to ensure that everything goes according to plan."

Jessica broke into a grin. "Thank you for the invite. If there is anything I can do to help—

I'm ready to jump right in."

Mary Ellen chuckled. "You might regret you said that."

She left Jessica to get settled in her workstation.

A brand-new laptop still in its packaging sat on her desk along with an iPhone. Mary Ellen seemed nice enough—she might enjoy working at the station, Jessica decided. She reminded herself that the only reason she was doing this was so that she could get closer to Traynor and Holt.

In Mary Ellen's office was a photograph of Holt and his family. "Is that your son?" she asked.

"Actually, he's my godson," she responded. "I love him like he was my own though."

"He has a beautiful family."

"Yes, he does. You will meet them at the event. Holt's father is the senior pastor at Bright Hope. Holt is the youth pastor."

Jessica pasted on a smile. "You're the second person to

tell me about that church. It must be a sign."

"I'm a member there. You should come visit us if you're looking for a church home."

"I'll definitely give it some thought."

Later that afternoon, she left work and drove straight to the mall. She had to find a dress to wear for the gala.

Jessica was in good spirits. She was one step closer to her family. Her mood darkened some over the fact that she would not be able to reveal herself to Holt and Traynor. She would just have to find a way to endear herself to them. She would not lose them a second time.

Chapter 14

"Pastor Deveraux…"

He stopped in his tracks at the sound of his name. Traynor was on his way back to Raleigh after speaking at a church in Maryland.

"It's me, Angela Saxon."

Traynor smiled at the sight of the well-dressed woman. "It's been a long time." Her shoulder-length hair was pulled back in a ponytail. She looked nice in the lilac-colored dress she wore.

"Yes, it has," she agreed. "I think the last time I saw you was right after William died."

"I miss my old friend."

"So do I," Angela said. "I was so sorry to hear about Jessie Belle."

"Where are you heading?"

"I'm flying to Raleigh. I was finally able to sell the house up here, so I'm back home for good."

"So you've put politics behind you?"

"I have a law office now. I heard you were over at Bright Hope, but I hadn't had a chance to visit."

"Once you settle in, I hope that you will find some time to join us one Sunday."

Angela smiled. "I'll make the time."

"We should get together for dinner sometime," Traynor suggested as they walked to the departure gate.

"I'd like that."

Traynor had never appreciated Angela's subtle beauty until now. He once believed there was no other women as exquisite as Jessie Belle. Her looks blinded him to her deeds. He wanted to marry again, but this time, he wanted a woman of substance.

Angela was married to a politician. She stood with him and they were a real team—everyone could see it. It was one of the things Traynor admired most when William was alive. He was a godly man who was vocal in his beliefs and through his tireless efforts, brought change to the triangle.

A high-profile lawyer in her own right, Angela seemed content to put her career on hold as she campaigned for her late husband, then played host to many charitable fundraisers.

"How are things going with you?" she asked.

"I'm still taking it one day at a time. My son is the youth pastor now at Bright Hope and I'm thrilled to be working with him in the ministry. He has a radio show and he produces several gospel concerts in the Triangle."

"Wow, he's a busy man."

Traynor agreed. "I sound like a proud father."

"You have every reason to be," she responded. "William always wanted a son, but we were not blessed with one. He loved our daughter though. We both loved her like crazy."

"I was sorry to hear of her passing."

"In the end, she tried to get her life together, but her mental illness…"

Traynor reached over and gave her hand a gentle squeeze. "We have all been touched by mental illness in one form or another. You and William put a face to it and I applaud your efforts in fighting for the rights of those who suffer from these disorders."

It was time to board the plane.

"I've enjoyed our conversation, Traynor. Here is my card. I'd like to stay in touch."

"Here is mine," he responded. "Why don't we make concrete plans for that dinner?"

Chapter 15

"**A**iden, what are you doing here?"

"I do go to the movies occasionally."

Chrissy glanced around to see if he had a date with him.

"I'm alone," he said, as if he knew what she had been thinking. "What about you? Did you come with someone?"

"I didn't."

"Since we're both here alone, can I convince you to at least have a cup of coffee with me?"

"Sure," Chrissy responded with a smile. She decided to stop running and allow herself the opportunity to get to know Aiden, especially since he was being so persistent. They had been talking for weeks now, and he was always a perfect gentleman.

They walked over to Starbucks which was in the same area as the movie theater.

"How are you enjoying your townhouse?"

"I'm loving it. I could use some help when it comes to decorating it though."

"Why don't you hire a professional?"

His eyes traveled to hers. "Do you give all men this hard of a time?"

"I'm not trying to give anyone a hard time, Aiden. I just don't have time for games."

"Neither do I," he responded. "Chrissy, I like you and I want to spend time with you. In the short time that we've been talking on the phone, I know that you are a woman of high moral standards."

She practically choked on her iced coffee.

"You okay?"

"Aiden, you don't know me."

"I'd like the chance to learn all about you."

"Then the first thing you should know is that I don't belong on a pedestal. I am about as flawed as they come."

"No one is perfect, Chrissy."

"I'm not apologizing for anything," she said. "I made some terrible choices in my past, but they led me to where I am now. I am not defined by my past."

"Are you going to leave me hanging?"

"I'm speaking to a group tomorrow evening at church. I'd like for you to come by. If you're still interested in having dinner with me after you hear what I have to say, then I'll say yes. However, if you decide to move on, then there's no hard feelings."

Aiden finished off his coffee. "I guess I'll be seeing you tomorrow."

He walked Chrissy to her car.

"I hope you can handle the truth."

"I'm looking forward to our first date."

Chrissy unlocked the door to her car and climbed inside. "Thanks for the coffee and conversation."

"Drive safe."

Aiden stayed on her mind during the entire ride home. She wondered if she were doing the right thing by allowing him to find out about her past in a room full of people. Chrissy decided this was the best way for her—she didn't know if she could do it one on one. She really liked him, but before she invested her heart in Aiden, she had to know that he could handle the truth about her former lifestyle and her ministry to help others get out of prostitution.

⁂

Aiden arrived just before Chrissy stood up to speak. She was nervous with him being in the audience, but she had to fight through the apprehension. She was walking in her calling and it was not something her feelings for him could get in the way of—when God called her to do this— she said yes. It was a covenant and could not be broken.

Chrissy walked to the podium. "I was someone who felt empowered by selling my body. I became a prostitute when I was sixteen years old. In my mind at the time, it was a smart business decision. I was in a group home and it was a way to make cash quick." She wouldn't allow herself to look in Aiden's direction.

"There were people from a church nearby who wanted to help me get off the streets, but I wasn't hearing it. The reason why is because you can't preach to a prostitute. I couldn't hear anything they had to say because my mind was on the streets. I had sex with dozens of men in a day.

103

I was arrested more times than I care to count… I never went to prison. I didn't realize it back then, but God's hand was on me. He kept me from serial killers, sadists and disease. I've been off the streets for almost three years now."

Applause sounded all over the room.

"… In Christ I found how to love myself, how to take care of my body and how to renounce things that damaged my body, that's how my transformation began… When someone is trying to change based on their own efforts, it's so easy to fail, but when someone seeks God and anchors themselves onto Him—it's different because He is the only one that can you help you."

When she finally dared to look in Aiden's direction, he was gone. Disappointment snaked down her spine, but she kept her composure. It was better to find out now rather than later.

Chrissy hung around for a few minutes after the meeting ended, but she couldn't wait to go home. At least she had some peanut butter fudge waiting for her.

She was surprised to find Aiden waiting outside beside her car.

Chrissy took a deep breath and exhaled slowly. "I'm glad you could make it."

"I was blown away by your testimony." He handed her a bouquet of flowers. "These are for you. I left out early so that I could grab these before the shop closed."

Her gaze stayed on his face. "I don't know what I was expecting to hear you say, but I know it wasn't that." This was the first time any man had ever bought her flowers and the gesture touched her deeply.

"Did you expect me to walk away from you?"

"It's a lot to handle, Aiden."

"I'm a man," he responded. "I can handle your past. The only thing I see is the woman you are now."

"I've never met anyone like you, Aiden."

"So, are we on for dinner?"

Chrissy broke into a smile. "Sure."

"How about tonight? I don't know about you, but I'm hungry."

"I'll follow you to the restaurant."

Aiden flashed her a dazzling grin. "The one I have in mind is just two blocks away."

Chrissy let out a squeal in her car. "Okay, don't get too excited. Let's just see where this goes." She turned on the ignition and followed him the short distance to the eatery.

꙳

"This is stunning," Chrissy said, setting her purse down in an empty chair. She loved the way the hydrangea and bougainvillea clustered at each end, filling pots and trailing up wrought iron scroll work attached to the walls of the Italian restaurant.

"And the food is delicious. Would you like wine?"

Getting comfortable in her chair, she glanced across at Aiden. He watched her rather than the scenery. "Yes, I'd like a glass of wine."

A waiter appeared as if by magic.

Aiden rattled off an order and the waiter disappeared into a circle of wait staff.

"You must eat here often. You didn't even look at the menu."

"It's a favorite of mine," he confessed. "You're going to love the shrimp scampi. It's some of the best I've had."

Chrissy couldn't get over how handsome he looked. Aiden seemed almost regal sitting at the table. He had a commanding presence about him. He was a man who knew exactly who he was.

The waiter returned with their wine, pausing to pour each a glass before retreating.

Aiden lifted his glass to scent the wine and give it a slow swirl. "Here's to two people getting to know one another and building a lifelong relationship."

Chrissy picked up her glass, brows lifted in challenge. "To us."

"I really like you."

She smiled. "Why?"

"I love your candor and your honesty. It's refreshing."

"I find that it cuts out a lot of unnecessary drama." Chrissy took a sip of her wine, finding it sweet and pleasant on the tongue.

Setting the glass down, she said, "Tell me more about yourself."

"I'm a single man who is looking to settle down. I have a good job and I'm a Christian. Dating is nice but I'm not interested unless it's leading to something serious."

"You might not want to say that too loud," Chrissy said. "You'll start a stampede over here."

He laughed.

"What do you do for fun?"

"I love sports. I like coaching basketball. I'm actually looking to join an AAU organization."

"You look very athletic so I'm not surprised." Even from across the table, Chrissy could smell his cologne.

The waiter brought their dinner— shrimp scampi, grilled zucchini and Caesar salad.

After Aiden blessed the food, Chrissy took several small bites of her meal. It was as good as he'd promised it would be.

"So what do you think?"

"I'm adding this to my list of favorite restaurants. In fact, I'm going to order shrimp scampi to go—it will be my lunch tomorrow."

"Do you have any plans this weekend?"

"I'm handing out safety packets Saturday evening. Outside of that I don't have anything planned."

"What are safety packets?" Aiden inquired.

"I put together some things that prostitutes can use like condoms."

"So you walk around looking for girls working?"

Chrissy nodded. "I pretty much know most of the tracks where they work."

"Are you in any danger?"

"No. All I'm doing is handing out the packets. I know a lot of the girls and guys. Back in my day, I wasn't in a stable. I was what you'd call a renegade girl. Nowadays, it not as safe to be out there without a pimp."

"Why did you decide to give up that life?"

"I started to hate myself. I hated what I was doing. Basically, I wanted more for myself."

"Is that when you reached out to God?"

Chrissy shook her head. "It took me a while to do that. I didn't feel like I was worthy. I wasn't clean and I didn't want to bring my dirt to the Lord. It took some time for me to understand that it is exactly what I should've done. That's what He wants us to do. Bring our filthy rags to Him."

They continued their conversation as they finished

their dinner. Chrissy found Aiden entertaining and interesting.

Afterward, Aiden walked Chrissy to her car.

"Dinner was wonderful. Thank you."

"The pleasure is all mine," he said.

Chrissy inclined her head. "Aiden, I look forward to getting to know more about you."

He grinned. "Same here. I really enjoy your company."

She drove away with a smile on her face.

Chapter 16

Clayton was home when Jessica arrived shortly after six p.m. "Did you get my text?"

He looked up from the paper he was reading. "About you working late? Yeah."

She sat her tote near the stairs, then joined him in the living room. "I volunteered to help out with stuffing the swag bags."

"Sounds like you're really enjoying your job."

"I am," Jessica responded. "Honey, you are not going to believe this... Mary Ellen has the same obsession that you have with those reef tanks."

"Really?"

She nodded. "I didn't really have a problem with her until she read my diary. However, I need her right now because she is my connection to Holt and Traynor. Clayton, my nieces and nephew are so adorable. I can't wait to meet them."

"Babe…"

"Don't say it," Jessica snapped. "I don't want to hear any negativity."

"I just don't want you getting hurt."

"I won't."

Clayton didn't respond.

"I want you to be my plus one for the gala the station is hosting," Jessica said, changing the subject, "It's time I introduce my fiancé to everyone."

"So you're saying that we're going public with our engagement? People will start asking you about the wedding date. What are you going to tell them?"

"Clayton…"

"I'm just saying."

Jessica embraced him. "You do know I'm going to marry you one day."

"I'd like it to be while we are young enough to still enjoy one another."

"Honey, the only difference in what we have now is a piece of paper."

"Call me old fashioned, but I want that marriage certificate."

"It's funny how things change," she said. "There was a time when all I could think of was being your wife." Jessica's eyes traveled to his face. "You weren't interested in settling down."

"Is this why you're stringing me along?"

She didn't like his tone. "Clayton, you know me better than that. I have always been honest with you about my feelings."

"And I've been truthful with you, Jess."

"You are the only man for me, Clayton. What's left of

my heart belongs to you."

"I love you."

Jessica kissed him. "I know," she whispered. She knew that he wanted her to declare her love for him in return, but it was something Jessica was not mentally prepared to do.

Chapter 17

Traynor slipped on a pair of trousers and a shirt. He was going over to Angela's house for dinner. They had been seeing each other since reconnecting on the flight. He found himself thoroughly enjoying Angela's company. They had a lot in common, but he admired her direct approach. She was up front about her desire to eventually marry again. Until seeing her, Traynor had not considered dating much less marriage, but Angela was captivating.

She was five years older than him, although no one could tell by looking at her. Angela exercised three times a week and lead a very active lifestyle. She had even convinced him to join her for early morning walks. Traynor liked most that she was nothing like Jessie Belle.

Chapter 18

"Frankie, thanks for inviting me over."

"Holt talks so much about you—I figured it was time you met the rest of the family."

Chrissy immediately felt comfortable in her presence. Frankie was very down to earth and very friendly.

"I love your hair," she said. "I'm a natural girl, too."

"I could never wear braids," Chrissy responded. "They didn't look right on me."

Frankie laughed. "Girl, my hair is so thick and unruly—I have to keep this stuff braided down. I don't want to scare anybody."

They laughed.

"I can't get over how everyone is so welcoming."

"I hate that Jessie Belle kept this secret. I'm sure it must have weighed on her."

"I didn't expect Jessie Belle to throw out the welcome mat. I just thought she'd be curious about her daughter."

"She once told me that she had so many regrets,"

Frankie said. "It was after she was paralyzed. Jessie Belle said if she had a do over, there was some people she would treat differently—two innocent victims. She talked about her past coming back to haunt her."

"You think she was referring to me and Reina?"

"I do. There was real pain in her eyes when she was talking that day."

"One of the reasons I've been so forthcoming about my life is because I've witnessed the effect secrets like this can have on a person's life. I can't help but wonder how things would've turned out if Anabeth Holt had just let Jessie Belle raise her children." Chrissy shrugged. "It's really no point in wondering because we will never know."

"I would like to think that things would've turned out for the better."

Chrissy smiled at Frankie. "So would I. Reina and I would've had a different life, that's for sure."

"Holt and I pray for her daily. We also pray for you."

"I need all the prayers I can get."

"Girl, you are doing some phenomenal work. I'd like to go with you sometime. Maybe the women's ministry at Bright Hope can partner with you."

"I'd love that."

Frankie rose to her feet. "I hear the girls. Are you ready to meet your nieces and nephew?"

Chrissy broke into a grin. "Yes. I feel like I've been waiting a lifetime."

Chapter 19

Jessica donned a black and silver gown for the gala. Her curly hair was long enough to slick back into a neat bun at the back of her neck. She walked out of the bedroom and downstairs when Clayton was waiting for her. He wore a black tuxedo with a silver vest and cummerbund.

"You look exquisite," he said.

"Thank you. I love seeing you in a tux."

He handed her a glass of wine. "So this pastor and everyone will be there tonight?"

"Yes, you will get to meet my family."

"No matter what happens, I need you to stay calm, Jess. Do not blow your cover."

"Have some faith in me, Clayton."

"Babe, I know how easily you can be provoked to anger."

"Tonight we are going to enjoy ourselves," Jessica assured him. "I will be on my best behavior."

She finished her wine, sat the glass on the table, then walked toward the door. "We don't want to be late."

"Jessica, I'm glad you were able to come," Mary Ellen said when they entered the ballroom. "There are some people I'd like you to meet."

She smiled. "Thanks for including me." Her eyes quickly traveled the room, searching. "This is my fiancé, Clayton Wallace."

Mary Ellen shook his hand. "It's a pleasure to meet you."

Jessica's eyes traveled the room. He was here. *Good.*

Mary Ellen escorted them over to where Traynor was standing.

Jessica gave Clayton a slight nod.

"I want to introduce you to my new assistant, Jessica Campana." To Jessica, she said, "This is Pastor Traynor Deveraux. He is a dear friend of mine and someone you'll see at the station from time to time."

He offered her a genuine smile as he held out his hand. "It's nice to meet you, Jessica."

"And you as well."

Traynor appeared to be studying her, prompting Jessica to wonder if he knew who she was on some level.

"So you're new to Raleigh?"

"Yes, I am," she responded.

"She's been living in New York for the past two years," Mary Ellen interjected.

"My fiancé's job brought him here to North Carolina."

"Well, it's certainly nice to meet you both."

Mary Ellen made several more introductions, but the only one Jessica cared about was Holt. He had been polite to her, but it was clear that his attention was focused elsewhere. She tried not to show her disappointment.

Seated at their table, Clayton said, "Babe, he doesn't know who you are."

Jessica folded her arms across her chest. "He didn't even take time to have a conversation with me."

"He's a radio personality. He's working. Give it some time."

She considered his words. "I suppose you're right. It just bothers me that my family is here and I can't tell them who I am."

"It wouldn't be wise." Clayton pulled her face to his, kissing her. "We're supposed to be engaged. Let's act like it."

"Look at the lovebirds," Natalia said as they approached the table.

Jessica pasted on a smile. "Hey lady. Don't you look stunning? Dean, it's good to see you."

They made small talk for a few minutes.

"Well, I guess we should get to our table. I'll call you over the weekend."

When Natalia and her husband walked away, Jessica uttered, "That witch is everywhere. There's no escaping her."

"You won't have to worry about her much longer."

Chapter 20

Standing nearby, Jessica watched as Chrissy and Holt shared a laugh over appetizers. The sight of the two of them together struck a bitter chord within her. Holt excused himself just as Sabrina approached Chrissy, saying, "I'm so glad you and your brother are getting to know one another."

Jessica practically choked on her drink. *Brother?*

She eyed Chrissy in confusion and shock.

"Holt seems to be a sweetheart," Chrissy said, "Frankie's really nice, too."

Jessica downed her drink and then ordered another. Her expression did not change, but deep inside, she was furious. Chrissy was passing herself as Jessie Bell's daughter.

And they believed it.

This had to be Natalia's doing. She had read her journal and fed the information to Chrissy—this was the only way their plan could work.

Jessica walked back to the table and said, "Let's take a walk."

"You're upset," Clayton stated.

"I have every right to be," Jessica responded. "That hooker over there is scamming the Deveraux family—she's stolen my birthright. I am not going to let her get away with it."

They walked outside and stood on the balcony.

The night insects were silent almost as if they could sense her fury. The temperature had dropped but in her anger, Jessica hardly noticed.

"I really want to make her pay. We have to do whatever possible to ensure she goes to prison, Clayton."

"There has to be motive when it comes to murder," Clayton stated. "You are missing that particular ingredient."

"No, I'm not," Jessica responded. "Mike and Natalia had an affair. When he refused to leave his wife—she killed him. When Charlotte figured it out, Natalia killed her, too."

"Not bad."

"All we need to do is plant a letter from Charlotte to Natalia accusing her of the affair."

"And her suspicions that Natalia was responsible for his death," Clayton interjected. "The justice system will do the rest."

"This is perfect. That witch will finally know how it feels to be rejected by the people who are supposed to love you."

"We need pictures of Natalia. Then we need to create a couple of emails and something with Charlotte's handwriting," Clayton said. "I know a guy who can forge the letter."

"I'm sure Martha has something with her daughter's handwriting." She paused a moment, then said, "At the boutique, she has memorabilia like Charlotte's yearbook, photos and I think letters. We just need someone to break in and get it. I can slip it into Natalia's house. I could hide it in one of the books in her office."

"Her filing cabinet might be a better place—easier for the police to find the letter."

Jessica considered his suggestion. "You might be right."

"You ready to go back inside?" Clayton asked.

She nodded.

Jessica touched the place where a tiny mole used to exist. She had to get rid of it as part of her disguise. She had gone through so much just to find Jessie Belle with the hopes of getting to know her mother, but the woman never gave her the time of day.

As much as she wanted to get to know her brother, Jessica envied the life Holt had—the love of his parents and a life of privilege. Her bitterness was rooted in the fact that she had been robbed of loving parents, a real home and family.

She looked around for Holt. He was seated at a table with his wife and father. There was a woman she didn't recognize beside Traynor. A smile tugged at her lips. Looks like he had forgotten all about Jessie Belle. *Good for you, Traynor.*

Her birth mother did not deserve the love of a man like him. He was too honorable and Jessie Belle too vile. Jessica thought about the conversation they had.

"Thank you for meeting me," Jessica stepped aside for Jessie Belle to enter the private room in the restaurant.

Jessie Belle was anything but impressed. "Why did you

want to meet with me?"

"There's something we need to discuss."

Jessie Belle sighed impatiently. "If you're going to black-mail me about the prostitutes, just do it. I'm not giving you a cent."

"You have this all wrong," Jessica stated, trying to put her at ease. "You were wronged a long time ago and I want to make things right."

She looked confused. "What are you talking about?"

"Your mother lied to you, Jessie Belle. You were told that your daughter died, but it wasn't true."

She gave Jessica a narrowed glinting glance. "I don't know what you're up to, but I only have one child and his name is Holt."

"I know that you were pregnant at sixteen," Jessica inter-jected. "It was your second pregnancy."

Jessie Belle gasped, but recovered quickly. "Then you should know that I aborted those pregnancies."

"You aborted one, but had to go through the delivery on the second."

"How do you know all this?" she demanded.

"Your mother had the midwife tell you that your daugh-ter died, but she didn't...I didn't die. Gloria raised me. She told me the truth of that night before she died."

Uncertainly crept into her expression. "I don't believe you."

"I'm your daughter."

"I know all about people like you. You found out some information about me and now you are claiming to be

my long-lost daughter. Reina, you have been trying to be a part of my world since the day we met. It's just not going to happen, dear. You will never be a part of my family."

"I am your family, Jessie Belle. I'm your daughter."

She would never plead and beg like that again, Jessica decided. She had poured her heart out to a woman who discarded her like trash only to be ridiculed.

I have the last laugh, Jessie Belle. Where are you now? Rotting in a grave with no one to mourn you. I'm alive and well. I will be a part of the Deveraux family—part of their legacy. There's nothing you can do about it.

❦

"Did you get any sleep at all?" Clayton asked when she walked into the kitchen. "You tossed and turned most of the night."

"No," she responded. "I kept seeing Jessic Belle's face. She was laughing at me and calling me pathetic." Jessica played with the belt on her robe.

He walked over and hugged her. "Why don't I make your favorite?"

Her mood brightened. "Chocolate chip pancakes?"

Clayton nodded. "Why don't you take a nice bubble bath and when you come back down, I'll have breakfast ready."

Jessica went upstairs and headed straight into the bathroom. She turned the water on and added lavender-scented gel beads.

She removed her robe and climbed inside of the tub. The hot water felt good against her skin. Jessica closed her eyes as she soaked in the bubbly liquid.

By the time she returned to the kitchen, Jessica felt more relaxed and in a good mood.

True to his word, Clayton had breakfast ready and

waiting for her at the table.

"What are you going to do today?" she asked, placing a napkin across her denim clad lap.

"I want to make some changes to my aquarium. I'm adding some new zoa."

Jessica shrugged. "I don't know why you and Mary Ellen find this stuff so fascinating. It's a bunch of rocks, plants and whatever else is in there."

"I find it relaxing," Clayton said as he sliced off a piece of sausage and stuck it in his mouth.

"Maybe I should help you? I'm looking for something to keep me relaxed."

"Make sure you put on gloves," Clayton instructed.

She looked over at him. "Why?"

"The zoa is very toxic."

"Are you serious?"

"Yes. According to Hawaiian legend, there was a time when fishermen began to disappear, some of the locals suspected a lone, hump-backed farmer was the murderer. When locals confronted him, they discovered that the hump on his back was the mouth of a shark fused to the man—they believed him to be a shark god. Nonetheless, they killed him, burned his body, and spread his ashes across the tide pool. Afterward, the water became toxic. The brown zoanthid in my tank was collected from that very location."

"So what happens if you touch it without gloves?"

"Probably nothing unless you have an open cut. It can be lethal if it gets into the blood stream. I've heard that boiling the rock with the zoa attached can also be dangerous."

Jessica chuckled. "Do you really believe that story?"

"Yeah, I do," Clayton responded. "Someone I know was trying to remove a species of zoa from the rockwork in his aquarium and boiled the rock to expedite the process. He developed a severe respiratory reaction and had to be taken to the hospital. He was told that if it had gotten in his bloodstream, he would have died."

"Maybe it was a different species."

"It's the same one. I had him frag some for me."

Jessica smiled. "How about giving me some for my boss? I'm sure she'd love it."

He eyed her.

"I'm just kidding, Clayton."

She filed away the information in the event, she needed it. Jessica made a mental note to search for more information on zoanthids. It just might prove to be useful.

❧

Natalia led Jessica into her office. "How do you like working for Mary Ellen?"

"It's good," she said. "I enjoy my job. It's not too demanding."

"I'm actually surprised that you wanted to do something so mundane. I'm sure you really don't have to worry about finances."

Jessica laughed. "That's what makes this fun for me. I like having my own money."

"I can understand that. That's why I'm going to work part-time. I want to open my own law firm eventually. Right now, I'm taking on a few clients." Natalia checked her watch. "As a matter of fact, I need to call one of my clients. First, I need to run upstairs for a second. Make yourself comfortable and I'll be right back."

"No problem."

Jessica rushed into the office, slipped the forged letter into a folder in the filing cabinet, and was back in her chair by the time Natalia returned.

"Sorry about that. I saw this shirt and it looked like you, so I bought it."

"You bought this for me?"

"Yes," Natalia responded with a smile. "I must confess that I don't usually get along with most women, but we really seemed to connect. I really cherish the friendship we're building."

Smiling, Jessica said, "I feel the same way."

Chapter 21

"Hello Aiden," Chrissy said, "I want you to meet a dear friend of mine."

She introduced him to Sabrina, who asked, "Have you been here before?"

"Today is my first time.," he said. "I've been visiting different churches in the area. I'm looking for a church home."

"Pastor Poolee is a wonderful teacher. We have a lot of different things going on in various ministries, and we are very active within the community."

His eyes traveled to Chrissy. "Sounds promising."

"Why don't you go inside and save a seat for me?" Chrissy suggested. She wanted a chance to talk to Sabrina before church services started.

"Girl, who is that?" Sabrina asked.

"Aiden St. Paul. I was his agent when he bought his townhouse and we've started having dinner together. We're building a friendship."

Sabrina shook her head. "No, it's a lot more than that, sweetie. I saw the way he was looking at you. Girl, you got a boo thang hanging onto your every word."

Chrissy laughed. "Whatever."

"I'm happy for you."

"Are things any better for you at the office?"

Sabrina's smile disappeared. "I quit last week. That jerk was going to tell my boss that I was a hooker."

"Why don't you just come work for us?" Chrissy suggested. "We need an office manager and you'd be good at it because you're so organized."

"Are you sure about this?"

"We can even pay you a real salary. If you're interested in selling real estate, I'll pay for you to take the class."

Tears filled Sabrina's eyes. "Do you think Patty will be okay with this?"

Chrissy nodded. "She and I already discussed it. I mentioned that you were thinking of leaving your old job."

"Natalia didn't want me to quit. She feels that I should file a lawsuit for sexual harassment, but who is going to listen to a former prostitute?"

"No weapons formed against you shall prosper—isn't that what you used to tell me?"

Sabrina chuckled. "Look at you... walking around quoting scripture. I do believe that one day I will be seeing you in the pulpit."

"I don't think so." Chrissy held Sabrina by the arm. "Praise and worship will be starting soon. Let's get inside."

Chapter 22

"Can I help you?" Natalia asked when she opened the door to two men dressed in suits. She had no idea why the police would be at her home. She stepped aside to let them enter. "What is this about?"

"I'm Detective Carson and this is my partner, Detective Lewis. We'd like to talk to you regarding the death of Pastor Michael Jennings and his wife."

"There was also an attempt made on my life as well by the same person."

"Yes ma'am," Detective Carson uttered. "Do you mind if we sit down?"

"We can talk in the living room." When they were all seated, Natalia inquired, "Why are you so interested in this case now? Has Reina done something else?"

"Some new information has come to light," Detective Lewis responded. "You knew both Michael & Charlotte Jennings, correct?"

Natalia nodded. "Yes. Charlotte and I were very close

friends. Their daughter Leah is my godchild."

"What was your relationship with Michael?"

She eyed Detective Carson. "I'm not sure what you're asking me. He and I were friendly. He was married to my best friend."

"Where were you the night Charlotte Jennings died?"

"I was home waiting for Charlotte to come over. She was going to stay at my home for a few days. She was afraid of Reina."

"You were home alone?"

"Yes, Detective Lewis. I was alone." Her lawyer instincts kicked in. "Which one of you is going to tell me what this is really about? I'm not the person you should be looking for—I was also a victim."

"We are just following up on new information," Detective Carson stated. "Thank you for your time." He rose to his feet.

His partner stood up as well.

Natalia escorted them to the front door. "I have nothing to hide, so feel free to come back anytime."

Although the detectives had gone, she still felt the stirrings of apprehension. Their sudden appearance did not feel right to her. It didn't help that they refused to give her any real information.

"The police were here earlier," Natalia announced when Dean arrived home that evening. "They wanted to know what my relationship was with Michael and Charlotte."

"Why now?"

"That's what I asked, but they didn't tell me anything other than they were following up on anew lead."

Dean embraced his wife. "Maybe they're getting close

to finding Reina."

"Or for some reason, they believe I'm a suspect."

He laughed. "I'm pretty sure that's not what they're thinking."

Natalia's instincts told her otherwise.

❦

"Detectives, you're back," Natalia said. Two days had passed since their last visit. They caught her just as she was about to head out for her standing Wednesday morning hair appointment.

"We have a warrant to search your place," Detective Lewis stated.

"Let me see it."

She scanned the legal document. "All you had to do is ask. As I told you before, I don't have anything to hide."

"We would like for you to stay in here, please."

"Whatever," she muttered. "Both my husband and I are attorneys."

"We are aware of that," Detective Carson responded.

Natalia fumed as men and women in uniforms searched through her possessions. Eventually, they began placing a few items in plastic bags. She wanted to scream for them to stop, although she knew that they were only doing their jobs.

"What are you looking for?" she asked.

Her question was met with silence.

"Detective Carson," one of the policemen called out. "In here…"

What in the world could he have found in my bathroom?

He walked out with a plastic bag containing a couple

of vials and several syringes.

"What is that?" Natalia asked.

"Why don't you tell me?" Detective Carson responded.

She shuddered involuntarily. "Whatever it is—it's not mine or my husband's. What is going on here?"

"I'm afraid we're going to have to take you down to the station. There's going to be more questions."

"I need to call Dean."

"You can call him on the way."

"I'm not riding in a police car," Natalia stated. "I will take my car."

Natalia could not believe that the police suspected her of killing Mike and Charlotte. She was in tears by the time Dean arrived.

"They think I'm a murderer."

"What proof do you have?" he asked the detective.

"We found the same drug that killed the pastor and his wife hidden in the bathroom downstairs."

Dean frowned. "That can't be. We purchased the house a month before we got married. I was the only one living there until after the wedding. This smells of a set-up to me."

"We received a tip from someone who said that we would find Natalia's stash of drugs somewhere in the house."

"And you believed it? It was probably Reina who called in this lie," Natalia said. "I don't know how she did it, but

I'm sure she is the one who planted the drugs. That's who you should be looking for."

"Did you check for fingerprints?" Dean questioned.

"Yes, but it just means that your wife wore gloves."

"I did nothing of the sort," she snapped. "I'm not a criminal."

Dean placed his hand on Natalia's shoulder. "Do you have a motive?"

"We believe that your wife and Pastor Jennings had an affair. When he refused to leave his family…"

Natalia laughed. "You have got to be *kidding*. Talk about reaching for the stars. I would never do something like that to Charlotte. Mike had an affair with Reina."

"Do you have proof of this alleged affair?" Dean questioned.

The detective did not respond.

"I'll take that as a no. Look, if you are not going to charge Natalia, then we're leaving."

"Mr. Anderson, there are photographs of your wife and the pastor." The detective looked straight at Natalia. "Compromising photos."

She gasped. "You're lying."

"'Fraid not."

"I want to see the photographs," Dean said.

A woman strolled in with a manila envelope. She laid them on the table, then left the room.

Detective Carson spread them on the table.

"That's not me."

"Sure looks like you, Mrs. Anderson. Look, I understand how these things can happen. I'm sure Pastor Jennings took advantage of you."

"Those pictures are fake," she uttered. "I never had an

affair with Michael. I'm being set up." She glanced over at Dean, whose expression was unreadable. "Honey, you can't believe this. Reina is trying to frame me for her crimes."

"Photographs don't lie."

Natalia folded her arms across her chest. "Really? So the photos in the *Enquirer* are real. I can answer that for you—*No, they're not.*"

"Is my wife under arrest?"

"You can take her home for now."

She rose to her feet. "Detective, I was almost killed by a mad woman. If she's capable of murder—don't you think she's smart enough to frame someone else for her crime? You are focused on the wrong person."

"Let's say you're right. Reina Cannon was also involved with Pastor Jennings. Maybe that's what the two of you were fighting about."

"I think you've missing your calling. You should be writing *Lifetime* movies."

In their car, Natalia turned to her husband, saying, "Dean, please tell me that you know I'm telling the truth."

"If the pictures are fake, they don't look like it."

"So you think I'm lying."

"I didn't say that, Natalia."

"But it's obvious that you don't believe me."

"Honey, did Jennings ever try to come on to you?"

"No, he was always a perfect gentleman around me. I was shocked when Charlotte told me that he'd had an affair. I didn't really know anything about the embezzlement until later."

"Did they ever find the money?"

"Not as far as I know," she responded.

"So if the cash wasn't found with Jenning's body, then

someone had to take it."

"That someone wasn't me. The only large sum of money I deposited came from the insurance company. I used it to repair the house before I sold it."

"We need to hire a specialist to prove that the photographs are fake," Dean said. "They are the only real evidence the detectives have to prove their accusation. If the photos were staged, then it's plausible that the drugs were placed in our house by Reina."

"If I ever see that woman again, there won't be a trial. I will kill her myself."

Chapter 23

Chrissy broke into a smile when Sabrina arrived. It was her first day working with her and Patty. "Good morning."

"Have you spoken to Natalia?"

"No," Chrissy answered. "Is everything okay?"

"The police think that she had an affair with Pastor Jennings. They think she may have killed him and Charlotte."

"If they think that—they don't know anything about Natalia. She wouldn't kill anyone for fear of breaking a nail."

"She thinks Reina is setting her up."

Chrissy straightened in her chair. *Was she back in town?*

"There's one more thing. The police searched her house and they found syringes and vials of drugs."

"How on earth could Reina have gotten into Natalia's house?"

Sabrina shrugged. "I'm just numb from the shock of all this. I thought that woman was gone from our lives forever."

"So did I."

"What did Natalia do to make Reina hate her so much?" Sabrina asked as she arranged her desk. "I mean; this woman wants my cousin in prison."

"She's out for revenge," Chrissy uttered. "We should check on Natalia. We can go during lunch."

Somehow she had to figure out a way to stop Reina. She was not going to let her sister hurt Natalia.

Chapter 24

"This is crazy," Mary Ellen uttered. She tossed the newspaper into the trash near Jessica's desk.

"Is everything okay?"

"I'm sorry. I just can't believe this nonsense about Natalia. She had nothing to do with the murders of Michael and Charlotte Jennings."

"She is a friend of mine," Jessica said. "I find it hard to believe myself. I was shocked when I heard the news."

"I know you haven't known her very long, but I assure you, Natalia is innocent. I believe I can prove it, too."

Jessica eyed her. "Really?"

Mary Ellen nodded. "The person responsible made a huge mistake. She wrote everything about her affair with the pastor down in a journal. I'm sure if I give it to the police—Natalia will be exonerated."

"A journal."

"Yes. It's very incriminating."

"Why didn't Natalia just hand it over to the police if she has it?"

"That's because she doesn't have it. I know where it is," Mary Ellen said.

Jessica waited for her to say more, but she didn't. She looked away to hide her irritation. "I think I'll drop in on Natalia during my lunch break. I want to see how she's holding up."

"Please give her my best," Mary Ellen said.

She muttered a curse when her employer walked away. Jessica wanted her journal back so that she could destroy it. Clayton had warned her against writing down such personal information, but it had been her only outlet for many years. Now she regretted it.

She desperately needed to find the journal. It held the key to her freedom. Although Mary Ellen did not say it, Jessica was sure that she had it. She was not going to let her turn it over to the police.

Jessica left at noon to visit Natalia.

"Thank you for coming over. It's so thoughtful of you."

"I've been worried about you since I heard the news."

"Everything is going to be worked out," Natalia said. "Despite everything, I have faith in the justice system."

Jessica grinned. "Spoken like a true attorney."

Natalia laughed, then grew serious. "I want you to know that I didn't do what the police are accusing me of—I'm being set up."

"I believe you. I know that you're innocent."

"You're a good friend, Jessica."

"And because I'm such a good friend, I bought lunch." She pulled a bag out of her tote. "I know how much you love *Jersey Mike's*."

"You brought me a Philly cheesesteak sub?"

Jessica nodded.

Natalia reached over and hugged her. "I am so lucky to have you as a friend."

The doorbell sounded.

"That's my cousin and my friend Chrissy," she said. "They wanted to come by to check on me. I'm glad you're all here."

"I actually need to get back to the office." Jessica didn't relish being around Sabrina and Chrissy—ex-prostitutes claiming to be Christians. Who would follow them to the throne of God? She had heard Mary Ellen discussing Chrissy's mission to get prostitutes off the streets.

She pasted a smile on her face when Natalia returned with Sabrina and Chrissy in tow.

"I saw you at the gala," Sabrina said after introductions were made. "It's nice to finally meet you."

"You, too."

She could feel the heat of Chrissy's stare.

Natalia told us that you've recently moved here. Where are you from?"

Jessica looked straight at Chrissy. "New York."

"You seem to pick up accents pretty fast," she responded. "You sound Southern."

"You think so?" Natalia asked.

Chrissy sat down in one of the accent chairs. "There's just a little hint of it."

"I grew up in Atlanta. Maybe that's why. However, most of my adult life has been in New York until now." Jessica rose to her feet. "I'm afraid I need to get back to the station."

"We'll have to get together for a girls' night," Sabrina

said.

"I'd like that."

Natalia escorted her to the door. "I hate you have to leave so soon."

"I'll give you a call later."

Jessica walked calmly to her car. She didn't like the way Chrissy kept staring at her. It was as if she were trying to see deep within. They had never spent time together, so there was no way Chrissy was smart enough to figure out that she and Reina were the same person.

Lucky for her.

⁂

"I'm definitely going to need some of that zoa to give to Mary Ellen." Jessica told Clayton. "She has my journal and she plans on turning it over to the police to clear Natalia. I'm not about to let that happen."

"What are they doing? Passing the journal around for everyone to read."

"They are trying to ruin my life."

"What are you going to do with the zoa?"

"I'm going to make sure that she gets it into her system. She's always getting paper cuts—I figure that's the best way. But I'm going to help her along by boiling the rock. We are working at her house tomorrow."

"Jess, this is nothing to play with. You have to be careful. This particular zoa produces a deadly toxin. It's the second deadliest poison in the world."

"I'll give it to Mary Ellen right before I leave her house." She folded her arms across her chest. "There is no way I'm going to let her help Natalia."

140

ֆ

Just before it was time for Jessica to get off, she said, "Remember I told you about my friend, the reef collector? Well, I thought you might like this. It will look beautiful with the collection you've put together."

Mary Ellen broke into a smile. "Thank you, Jessica. These are beautiful."

"I can help if you'd like, although I wouldn't know the first thing about any of this."

"Join the club," she responded with a chuckle.

Jessica pointed to the band aid on Mary Ellen's finger. "Another papercut?"

"Actually, I was trying to fix my stapler and I stuck myself."

"Why don't you let me handle stuff like that? You're going to do some serious harm if you keep this up."

They laughed.

"If you don't need me, then I'm going to head home." Jessica grabbed her tote.

"This I think I can handle," Mary Ellen said.

"Okay, I'll see you tomorrow."

During the drive home, Jessica gave Natalia a call.

"Hey Sweetie … I was just calling to see how you're doing."

"I can truly say that I've had better days. I went down to the police station to see if there was any new evidence. They are trying to pin those murders on me. It's really frustrating."

"I'm sure. How about I come pick you up and we can have dinner. We could go to Bonefish Grill. I know it's one of your favorite places to eat."

"I'm not really hungry."

"Natalia, you need to keep up your strength. All this mess will clear itself up. I'm sure of it."

"I know, but it's just frustrating to even have to deal with the drama. If I had a gun, I'd hunt that evil witch down and just shoot her in the face."

Jessica choked back her laughter. Natalia wouldn't do anything but beg for her life.

"Maybe having dinner out will help take my mind off everything. Dean is in Charlotte and won't be home until tomorrow afternoon."

"I'm on my way to your place. I should be there in about fifteen minutes."

"I'll be ready."

Her next call was to Clayton.

"I just wanted to let you know that I'm taking Natalia to dinner at Bonefish Grill. Dean is away for the night. Send Nikko and Miguel over there to make it look like someone broke in. Tell them not to take anything. Natalia feels a little too comfortable. I just want to shake her up a bit."

"Okay, but make sure you go inside the house with her afterward. You make the call to the

Police, but make it clear that you didn't go in the house beforehand. Then they might consider that Natalia tore up her own house."

"To throw them off the trail."

"Right."

"I just hope she doesn't fall apart on me," Jessica said. "I'm wearing a silk blouse and I don't want her sobbing all over it."

"Make sure you have plenty of tissue on hand, in that case."

Jessica laughed. "She does look like she can cry a river."

❦

"I wish Dean had come home instead of staying in Charlotte."

"Do you want me to come inside with you? I'll stay a while if you want some company."

She seemed relieved. "I'd like that."

When she opened her front door, and stepped inside, Natalia stared at disarray that used to be her living room.

"Was it like this when you left?" Jessica asked.

Backing away, Natalia shook her head. "Somebody was in my house... oh Lord, they might still be here. We need to leave."

"Let's go back to the car," Jessica suggested. "I'm calling the police right now."

"Maybe we should park down the street." Natalia was trembling all over.

Fighting back laughter, Jessica drove a few yards away from the house, and then shut off the car.

"I knew she was back. I told Dean that she had come back, but he didn't believe me."

"Sweetie, who are you referring to? Who is she? That Reina person."

"Yes. She's the one who's framing me."

"Are you sure?"

"Just as sure as you and I are sitting in this vehicle. *Reina is back and she's out to get me.*"

"The police should be here any minute."

Natalia looked as if she wanted to cry. "Why won't she just leave me alone?"

"You can tell me to mind my business, but what did you do to this woman?"

"I took her journal because I suspected she killed my friend and her husband. I wanted to prove that she was a murderer."

"Maybe you shouldn't have taken something like that," Jessica offered. "Why don't you just give it back to her?"

"I wanted to stop Reina before she hurt another person. She is such a cold, calculating …" Natalia shook her head. "Her mother wasn't a nice person, but Reina—she makes Jessie Belle look like an angel."

Jessica chewed on her bottom lip to keep from slapping Natalia's face. *How dare she try and compare me to Jessie Belle Deveraux. I am nothing like her.* She kept looking straight ahead as she struggled to retain her outwardly calm composure.

"If I were you, I'd just give her the journal. Don't take this the wrong way, Natalia, but you have encountered some lethal people. Are you sure you don't have a target on your back?"

"I don't have the journal anymore," Natalia said. "I gave it to someone else that she was stalking for lack of a better word. She was fixated on this family and I thought they needed to know the truth."

The police arrived before Jessica could utter a response. "I guess we should get out so you can talk to them."

"Jessica, please don't leave just yet?"

She smiled. "I won't. I've already texted Clayton to let him know that I'm here with you."

"Thank you for being my friend."

If only you knew how I really felt about you, Natalia.

She had pretty much confirmed what Jessica already

knew. Mary Ellen had the journal.

Chapter 25

"Do you believe that Natalia is guilty?" Angela inquired as they settled down in her family room.

Traynor shook his head. "No. This reeks of Reina. Apparently, she must be back in town."

"Are you worried?"

"She doesn't want to hurt me or Holt. However, she did try to kill Natalia."

"And you really believe that she's the one trying to frame her?"

"Reina believes that Natalia poses a threat to her," Traynor said. "If Jessie Belle had handled things much differently…maybe the poor girl wouldn't have done the things that she did."

"Blame falls on Reina as well," Angela said. "She made certain choices that landed her in this situation. From what you've told me, Jessie Belle didn't know she had given birth to twins."

"She was a smart woman. When they each came to her, she should've figured it out. Chrissy brought DNA results, but Jessie Belle was only interested in preserving the lies she'd told."

"She didn't want to lose you, Traynor."

"I can't say how I would've responded back then, but I wasn't given the opportunity to make up my own mind."

"I can't begin to imagine what you must be feeling."

"Angela, I'm angry. Jessie Belle did a lot of things to hurt people. Don't get me wrong—she tried to turn her life around and I believe that she was truly repentant before she died. I just never realized until after her death, just how many lies she told.

"William was no saint either. His mistress came to the funeral."

Traynor was surprised. "Jessie Belle was faithful during our marriage as far as I know. I know that I'm far from perfect, but I have tried to live my life as God ordained. However, I am struggling to get rid of the anger and bitterness I feel toward Jessie Belle."

"In time, you will be able to do that," Angela said. "I never thought I could forgive William for cheating on me, but one day I woke up and realized that he was dead. He would have to stand before God on judgement day for his sins."

"You're right. I need to let this go."

Traynor left for home two hours later.

That night he went to bed troubled. It was hard for him to move past his anger. It was past midnight when he drifted off to sleep.

"*Traynor, I've missed you.*"

Confused, he turned around at the sound of that familiar sing-song voice. "*Where am I?*"

"*Anywhere you want to be. Aren't you happy to see me?*"

"*No, I'm not, Jessie Belle.*" *She was once again that beautiful, ethereal angel he met all those years ago. She hadn't aged in death.*

Her smile disappeared. "*What did I do now?*"

"*You lied to me from the very beginning. You weren't a virgin.*"

"*This is why you look so sad—so disappointed in me. Because I wasn't the pure bride you thought me to be. My mother convinced me to deceive you, Traynor. She didn't think someone like you would want a girl who had been sexually active. I knew that you loved me and I believed you would have accepted me.*" *She shook her head.* "*Mama thought she knew everything.*"

"*If you believed in me, then why didn't you tell me the truth after we got married?*"

"*I just figured I'd leave well enough alone. It was a bad move; I see that now.*" *Jessie Belle reached out to him.* "*Traynor, I never lied about my feelings for you. I love you.*"

"*I feel as if I don't know you at all.*"

"*Trust your heart. Everything I did was for you—well for our family.*"

"*What about your daughters, Jessie Belle? What about them?*"

"*Daughters?*"

"*You gave birth to twins, Jessie Belle.*"

Tears formed in her eyes. "*Mama lied to me. She told me that my baby died. She never said there were two … so I did hear my child cry that night.*"

"How could you so easily dismiss their claims? All they wanted from you was acceptance."

"Chrissy was a hooker. You never would've accepted her. Reina, I think she's more like me—you didn't need that in your life."

"Reina is worse," Traynor said. "She's killed people."

"She pushed me ..."

"No, that was Chrissy."

Jessie Belle released a soft gasp. "Payback for Miami."

"Things would've turned out different if you'd just talked to me. We could've worked this out."

"I wanted to come to you, Traynor, but I was scared. I didn't want to lose you."

"Talk to me now, Jessie Belle. Help me understand."

"I made a lot of mistakes. I told lies which only led to more lies—it worked for Mama. She actually convinced my dad that I was putting on weight. She told him that I was still a virgin. She hated that I was in love with a white boy—she feared what his family would do if they found out. I figured if I had a child, then everyone had no choice but to accept our relationship. Mama didn't give me a choice when it came to my pregnancies—she said that my daddy would hate me if he found out. I wanted my babies, but I loved my daddy."

"I don't understand how your mother could've done this."

"None of us are perfect, Traynor."

He nodded in agreement.

"Can you forgive me?"

"I'm trying. It's just a lot to take in."

"Unforgiveness is a sin."

He eyed her. "I know."

"I need you to do something for me. I know I have no right to ask, but I'm doing it anyway."

"What is it?"

"Save my daughter. Break the Holt generational curse."

"Jessie Belle... I forgive you."

She smiled. "I know. Only a godly man could forgive someone like me. My daughters need you in their life. It is because of me that they are ..."

"Chrissy is on the right track. She helps prostitutes who want to get off the streets."

Jessie Belle seemed surprised. "Wow. That's not the same girl I knew."

"No, she's not. I think you'd be proud of her."

"Promise me that you will be there for all of my children."

"Are there anymore that I need to know about?"

She laughed. "No more secrets. Although you didn't know some of the stuff I did—I laid all of my sins before the Lord and repented. I do want you to know that I never lied about loving you."

Traynor could see the truth in her eyes.

"You are a good man. Go live your life to the fullest. Find an amazing woman who deserves you."

Traynor sprang up in bed.

He glanced over at the clock. It was almost three in the morning. The dream seemed so real, so vivid. Traynor sniffed the air. He could smell her perfume.

He shook away the notion that any of this could be real. It was nothing more than a dream, but one tangible enough to wipe away all the anger he'd felt for Jessie Belle from his heart.

Chapter 26

The following day, Mary Elle groaned in pain as she placed a hand to her chest. They were just about to have a meeting regarding some changes in programming.

Jessica was instantly by her side. "Oh my goodness. Are you okay?"

"I'm having chest pains... and... t-trouble breathing..."

"I'm calling the paramedics."

She pretended to call to delay their arrival. Clayton told her that death could possibly come in minutes or hours. Mary Ellen didn't look well at all.

"I'm calling again." This time she actually made the call.

"They should be here shortly."

Jessica brought Mary Ellen a glass of water. "Here you go..."

Paramedics rushed in and took over.

"I'll get your purse," she said. Jessica needed the key to Mary Ellen's house so that she could search for the journal.

"Do you want me to come to the hospital with you?"

"Call Traynor, please."

"I'll call Holt as well," Jessica said. She handed the purse to one of the paramedics. "I think her medical information is on her phone."

She left the station a few minutes later.

Clayton pulled up in his car just before she did. "What's going on?"

"Mary Ellen is at the hospital."

"Why didn't you go?"

"I figured it was better that I not be there."

"You might be right. So what happens now?" he asked.

"I'm going over to her house as soon as it gets dark. I need to find that journal."

"I'll go with you."

Jessica smiled. "Great. I won't feel entirely free until it's back in my possession."

Chapter 27

Mary Ellen waved Traynor into her room. "How are you feeling?"

"H-Horrible," Mary Ellen mumbled weakly. "They took some blood for testing, but they said I wasn't having a heart attack."

"Angela said that she'll be by later to visit you."

Mary Ellen shifted her position. "How are things... between you two?"

"Great," Traynor responded as he pulled a chair closer to the bed. "She is a wonderful and caring woman. I really enjoy her company."

Mary Ellen started to pant.

"What's wrong?" Traynor asked.

"I can't breathe..."

He pushed the call button and said, "We need a nurse in here. *Hurry.*"

Traynor began to pray. "Heavenly Father, You are the

One I turn to for help in moments of weakness and times of need. I ask you to be with your daughter Mary Ellen in this illness. Psalm 107:20 says that you send out your Word and heal. In the name of Jesus, drive out all infirmity and sickness from her body. Please restore her to full health, dear Father. Amen."

When he opened his eyes to look at Mary Ellen, Traynor whispered, "Dear Lord, I ask you to turn my sorrow into joy, and pain into comfort for others. I will trust in your goodness and hope in your faithfulness, even in the middle of this suffering."

The nurse rushed in and immediately began checking Mary Ellen's vitals. A doctor burst into the room seconds later.

Traynor was ushered out of the room while the medical staff fought to save her.

Ten minutes later, the doctor walked out. His expression grim as he approached Traynor, who said, "I know she's gone."

"We did everything we could to revive her."

He nodded. "I'm sure you did. Mary Ellen lived a good life—she was a good person. I have no doubt that she is with the Lord."

"As soon as I have more information, I'll let you know."

Traynor gave a slight nod. "Thank you, doctor."

He walked down to the hospital chapel and sat on the first row. "I don't know why this happened, Lord. I don't understand why you chose to take Mary Ellen... what good will come out of this tragedy?

※

"Do you know what happened?" Holt asked his father as soon as he arrived to the hospital. Traynor was waiting for him in the waiting area. He gestured for his son to sit down.

"Why did she die?"

"Apparently, it was accidental palytoxin poisoning." The doctor had just informed him of the test results minutes before he came down to meet his son.

Holt frowned. "What on earth is that?"

"You know she had that aquarium full of stuff. Well, some of whatever was in there was toxic. It got into her bloodstream somehow."

"This can't be happening."

"I'm afraid it is, son. Mary Ellen is gone."

"She was so excited about this new hobby of hers," Holt said. "Now she's dead because of it. Dad, it just doesn't make any sense to me."

"I choose to believe that God needed another angel in heaven and called her home."

"I don't want to lose another person."

Traynor embraced his son. "We will get through this somehow."

Chapter 28

"Where is it?" Jessica was filled with white hot fury. "We have looked everywhere."

"Calm down."

Her gaze snapped to his. "I can't calm down, Clayton. I need to find my journal before someone finds it."

She picked up a plate and tossed it across the room.

"Jess, stop it. I need you to calm down."

"I'm too angry."

"We need to get out of here."

Her cell phone rang.

Jessica looked over at Clayton and said, "It's Holt."

"You should answer it."

"Hello, this is Jessica."

"Hey, this is Holt Deveraux. I'm at the hospital."

"How is Mary Ellen?"

"I'm afraid it's not good. She's gone, Jessica."

"Excuse me?"

"She didn't make it."

"Holt, I'm so s-sorry to hear t-this." She pretended to sound broken up.

"The administrative offices will be closed for the rest of this week. I just wanted you to know."

"Is there anything I can do to help, just let me know."

"I'll give you a call later in the week."

"Holt, I'm sorry for your loss."

She hung up and said, "We need to get out of here. I don't know if anyone will come by the house. I also need to get her keys back with her things."

"I'll clean up the broken pieces of that plate, then we can leave."

"I'm going to offer to help pack up her things. She must have my journal hidden somewhere like a safe deposit box."

"You're really not going to give up on this."

"Clayton, you know me better than that. I'm not going to quit until I get everything I want."

Chapter 29

Mary Ellen was dead.

Natalia was saddened by the news, although they were never what she considered close. She turned off the radio and was about to go upstairs when her husband called out to her.

"Honey, I was going through the files in the office and I found this." Dean handed Natalia a letter.

"I… I never saw this," she murmured.

"Is that Charlotte's handwriting."

"Dean, you have to believe me. She never gave me this letter. Charlotte knew that Mike and I weren't lovers. She never once accused me of something like this."

The guarded expression on his face showed that he wasn't convinced she was telling the truth. "So you're saying that someone came into this house and planted the note from Charlotte."

"Reina had someone from the police department put

it here—that's the only explanation. I know she is behind this."

"We need to give this to the police."

"Dean, I'll be arrested."

"Honey, this is the only way we can find out the truth. If you're right, then we will be able to prove that the letter is a forgery."

"I'm just not sure we can trust the police. I don't know who Reina has in her pocket."

"Where is your faith, Natalia?" Dean asked. "No weapons formed against you shall prosper. I believe that we will be able to prove your innocence."

"God knows the truth. What I need to know is if you believe me. Do you?"

"I don't think that you're capable of murder."

"But you're not sure about the affair," Natalia interjected. "You actually think this letter is real."

"If you look me in my eyes and tell me that you weren't involved with Michael Jennings, I'll believe you."

She met his gaze with her own. "Mike and I never had an affair."

❧

"This letter was found in a file cabinet in our office." Natalia looked Detective Carson straight in the eye. "It's a forgery. Reina is trying to frame me for crimes she committed. Have the letter tested and you'll find that I'm telling the truth."

Dean produced another packet. "These are samples of Charlotte's handwriting. They were given to us by her mother."

"And if we find the letter is real?"

"I can't even consider the possibility," she responded. "Detective, we came to you with this evidence. If I were guilty, do you really think I'd be sitting here?"

"What do you believe will be Reina Cannon's next move?"

"She wants me behind bars," Natalia said, "I don't believe she'll stop until I'm arrested."

"So if that doesn't happen…"

"Then I'm sure she is going to find a way to come after me."

"Why are you on her radar?" Detective Carson inquired.

"Charlotte came to me with her suspicions that Reina and Mike were lovers. The night she died, Charlotte was coming to stay with me because she was afraid. I confronted Reina after she died—I told her that I'd gone to Florida and knew that she had been there with Mike."

"My wife and I look forward to hearing from you regarding the letter." Dean rose to his feet. "Sweetheart, we're leaving if there's nothing more."

"I'll be in touch," Detective Carson said.

Natalia waited until they in the car before asking, "Do you think he believes us?"

"Actually, I do. Otherwise, you might have been arrested."

Chapter 30

"I'm sure you heard about Mary Ellen?" Jessica asked. She and Natalia met for lunch.

"It was on the radio all morning. How are you taking all this?"

"I haven't known her very long, but she was a really nice person."

"Mary Ellen could also be a witch," Natalia said with a tiny smile. "When we first met, I couldn't stand her and the feeling was mutual. Our relationship changed after a while…"

"Natalia, what's going on with your friend's case? Do they still think you had something to do with it?"

She gave a slight shrug. "If they do, then hopefully, they will discover the truth soon."

Jessica wasn't satisfied with Natalia's response, but decided not to push for answers. She was shocked that she hadn't been arrested already.

"I wonder what's going to happen to the radio station," Natalia murmured.

"I've been thinking about the same thing. Everyone is in shock right now. I know that I am."

"Does anyone know how she died?"

"Not really. They said it had nothing to do with the flu, however."

"I'm not completely convinced that Mary Ellen died of natural causes." Natalia shifted in her chair.

"You think this has something to do with that woman… what's her name again?"

"It's Reina and yes, I think she might be involved."

"For what reason?"

"Jessica, that woman is a psychopath."

❧

Jessica entered the house like a tornado. She tossed her purse, uttering a string of curses, and stormed upstairs into the master bedroom.

Clayton walked out of the bedroom. "What is wrong with you?"

"I just had lunch with Natalia," she shrieked. "She hasn't been arrested. What is taking them so long?"

"Jess, calm down…"

"This is not going according to plan." She picked up a pillow and tossed it across the room. "I'm getting tired of that witch calling me every kind of evil out there. Today she said I was a psychopath."

"She doesn't know you like I do," Clayton responded. "Besides, it doesn't matter what she thinks."

"She should be in jail."

"Be patient, Jess. It's coming."
"It better."

Chapter 31

Chrissy sat down at the table with Sabrina and Natalia. "Traynor said she died because some of the plants or whatever they are in her aquarium was toxic."

Natalia frowned. "Why would she have something like that in her home?"

She shrugged. "I don't think she knew that they could kill her. This was something new that she was doing."

"This must be a new trend. Jessica has a huge one at her house and it's filled with exotic looking plants and coral reefs."

"I never even wanted a fish," Sabrina said. "I'd rather have a puppy, then deal with an aquarium. Too much maintenance."

Chrissy laughed. "Having a dog is like raising a child."

She glanced over at Natalia, who seemed to be distracted. "Hey you."

"I'm sorry. I was just thinking about everything that's happened." Natalia looked at her friends. "I don't know how she did it, but Reina has been in my house. She even managed to plant a letter in my file cabinet. She wants the police to believe that I'm the one they should arrest. Dean says that he believes me, but I'm not sure that he really does."

Sabrina reached over, covering her hand. "I'm so sorry that you're having to deal with this."

"I'm still holding out that the truth will prevail," Natalia said. "I really hate Reina."

Chrissy did not respond.

"I know she's your sister, but she has made my life miserable. I'm a newlywed. Dean and I shouldn't be worrying if I'm about to end up in prison. We've been trying to have a baby…" Natalia's eyes filled with tears. "I don't know how much more of this I can take."

"I will do everything in my power to keep Reina from hurting you," Chrissy said. "I've gone by the salons, and they have a new owner. I've been looking for her."

"She's a lot smarter than I initially gave her credit for," Natalia said. "I tried to protect Traynor and Holt, but I really wish I'd just stayed out of all that drama."

"For what it's worth, I think you did the right thing," Chrissy replied. "I would've done the same thing."

"She's not after you, Chrissy."

"Not yet, but that may soon change once she finds out that I'm looking for her."

The next day, Chrissy went back through the records of the hair salons that were once owned by Reina Cannon.

"After Reina left, the businesses were purchased by a person named Clayton Wallace. He then sold one to a Helen Jacobs and the other to Marc Thompson."

"They were in foreclosure up until Wallace bought them," Sabrina said.

"It's interesting to me, that they were purchased by the same person. They didn't go to auction at the same time," Chrissy murmured.

"So you think that the person who bought them, knew Reina?" Sabrina asked.

"It's possible."

"Okay, so let's say that this person is a friend of hers. What now?"

Chrissy shifted her position in the chair. "She's here in Raleigh or very close by. If what we're thinking is true, then she has money."

"How do you think she was able to get into Natalia's house?"

Chrissy looked at Sabrina. "What if she walked right through the front door?"

"I don't understand."

"She met Jessica right before all of this stuff started happening, right?"

Sabrina nodded. "You think she is a friend of Reina's?"

"There's something about her that has always bothered me. I just can't put my finger on it."

"Do you think we should mention any of this to Natalia?"

Chrissy shook her head. "I don't want to say anything until I have concrete proof. I'd rather not get her hopes up."

Chapter 32

It seemed like the entire Triangle turned up for Mary Ellen's funeral. Jessica wanted Clayton to attend with her, but he refused. He hated funerals, especially the ones where the police turned out in crowds. Mary Ellen was well-respected and loved by many. She sat on too many boards for Jessica to remember.

She glanced to her left. Chrissy was seated with Sabrina.

I wonder if those two go to the bathroom together?

The thought made her smile.

When Traynor and Holt walked in behind Mary Ellen's family, Jessica struggled to remain seated. She wanted so much to comfort her brother. He had not taken her death very well.

Jessica felt a moment's regret at causing Holt so much pain.

It was necessary, my dear brother. She left me no other

choice. Maybe one day you'll understand that all I did was because I wanted you in my life.

Natalia and Dean were seated in another part of the sanctuary. She hoped to leave before they saw her. Jessica wasn't in the mood for her constant chatter. She didn't know how much longer she could stand being around Natalia, the person she hated most.

When Jessica glimpsed Martha, she felt a thread of guilt. She hated having to kill Charlotte. She didn't like leaving little Leah alone to grieve the loss of both parents. She never wanted to do something like that to a child—children were innocent little creatures. Charlotte was responsible for her own fate, however. If she'd just kept her mouth shut—she would still be alive.

Chapter 33

After the funeral, Chrissy invited Natalia and Sabrina over to her house. She decided to come straight home instead of going to the repast. Dean had a meeting, so it would only be the three of them.

"I still can't believe that Mary Ellen is gone," Natalia stated as she placed her purse on the hall table. "We weren't what you would call friends, but for the past year, we could be in the same room without throwing shade. Poor Holt... he loved his godmother."

Chrissy agreed. "He's not taking her death very well."

"Who was the woman with Traynor?" Sabrina inquired.

"Angela Saxon," Natalia responded. "She was married to Congressman Will Saxon."

"Okay, I thought she looked familiar."

"What do you know about Jessica?" Chrissy asked. "You two have been spending a lot of time together."

"Oh, Jessica is a sweetheart." Natalia looked. "We actually have a lot in common."

"Does she come to the house often?"

"Not really. She is engaged to be married. Between her job at the station and wedding plans, she doesn't have a lot of time for recreation. We try to meet for lunch at least once a week. And she's been super supportive during all of the drama with the police."

Chrissy did not ask any more questions. She didn't want to rouse any suspicions in Natalia. "I'm glad to hear that you have Jessica in your corner."

"She has been a wonderful friend. *Trust me*, she is nothing like Reina."

"If Reina was here," Sabrina said, "I'm sure she's gone by now. The police are still looking for her so it's not like she can just walk around town without someone noticing."

"I wouldn't put anything past her." Chrissy rose to her feet and walked over to the window, peering out. "When you're hungry for revenge… you'll take risks to fulfill that hunger." She glanced back at them. "I know from experience."

"I guess that's why she's trying to frame me," Natalia stated. "I don't want to ever tangle with that woman again, but I'm not going to let her railroad me to prison."

"She's angry and she needs—"

"She needs Jesus," Sabrina interjected. "Reina definitely has some loose nuggets in the brain and a zero conscience."

"Regardless, she is still my sister." Chrissy turned her attention back to the goings on outside. "No matter what, I'm not going to abandon her."

"Girl pleeeze," Natalia uttered. "Don't bother wasting

your time. If she knew that you were her twin, she'd be trying to get rid of you."

Chapter 34

"Do you mind if I join you?"

Chrissy looked up from her tablet. "Not at all."

"How is your day going so far?"

"Let's see…" she checked her watch. "It's eight-thirty in the morning. So far so good." Chrissy chuckled. "Hey Aiden…"

He grinned. "Got any plans for tonight?"

"No. What's up?"

"Why don't we have dinner and then go to that jazz club downtown," Aiden suggested.

"Sounds like a plan, she murmured.

"I'd like for us to go to Wilmington this weekend. I rented a condo and don't worry, it has two bedrooms."

"You know how much I love going to the beach."

"I enjoy it as well," Aiden said. "I can't wait to explore

the outer banks."

"Maybe we'll do that next month," Chrissy responded.

After the conversation ended, she sat at her desk thinking of how her life had turned for the better. Chrissy decided it was time to tell Aiden that she was bipolar. She didn't want there to be any secrets between the two of them.

In the months that they'd been spending time together, Chrissy found that she was falling hard for Aiden. She enjoyed their lengthy conversations on the phone or face to face in the evening. She felt a bottomless peace where he was concerned. Chrissy believed that God had sent this wonderful man to share her life with him.

They were a perfect fit.

God had done so many amazing things in her life. Chrissy closed her eyes and sent up a prayer for her sister. She wanted Reina to experience a loving and generous God. She wanted her to know that despite everything, God loved her.

"It's official. Aiden and I are in a committed relationship." Sabrina's car was in the shop, so Chrissy offered to pick her up.

"Praise the Lord," Sabrina screamed.

"Girl, whatever. *Anyway*, we are going on our first romantic getaway this weekend."

"Oh really…"

"We're staying in separate bedrooms."

"If you say so."

Chrissy laughed. "I can't with you…"

"I'm just being real," Sabrina said. "The struggle can

be real sometimes. That's why I bought this purity ring. I needed a tangible reminder to keep me on the right path."

"Maybe I should get one. Aiden hasn't even brought the subject up—it makes it easier, but when I'm with him... my mind tries to take me there."

"Chrissy, I have a confession to make. I don't know if I could be as honest as you have with Aiden. I don't think there are many men out here as understanding as he is."

"I wanted him to hear it from me. I'm out there trying to help prostitutes, so Aiden needed to know the truth." Chrissy glanced over at her. "When you meet the right man, he'll understand. You don't have to tell anyone until you're ready."

"We have worked hard to change our lives. I just don't think we should be penalized for our sins of the past."

Sabrina, you once told me that we shouldn't allow ourselves to be defined by other's opinions."

"I know. It's just that jerk got under my skin. He really thought of me as nothing but some cheap hooker. That's all he saw when he looked at me."

"That's not who you are, Sabrina. He probably has no respect for women period. Don't let his issues become your problem. You left the company and you don't have to deal with him anymore."

"Maybe not, but there are others in the world like him."

"Everyone has a past," Chrissy said. "I own mine and I won't walk around in shame any longer. I am a daughter of the Most High. I am above and not beneath ..."

"*Preach* girl."

Not too long ago, Chrissy felt the same way and it was Sabrina who introduced her to the Heavenly Father, she now served.

❧

Aiden had tickets to a play and invited Chrissy to join him. The more time she spent with him, the more she believed that he was the perfect man for her. She loved his personality and positive outlook on life in general. He was also a romantic.

When he arrived to pick her up, Aiden brought her roses. This time they were red.

"I thought I'd surprise you with something just as beautiful as you are," he told her with a grin.

"Thank you, Aiden. They are stunning." Chrissy took them to the kitchen and placed them in a vase.

She grabbed her purse and they left for the play. Afterward they had a late dinner before returning to the house.

Aiden pulled her into his arms, kissing her. "I've been waiting to do that from the moment you opened the front door." Chrissy reached up and stroked his cheek. "I really enjoy your company, Aiden. I want you to know that I truly care for you."

"That's good to hear," he responded. "Because I'm in love with you."

"Aiden…"

He stopped Chrissy from completing her sentence by covering her mouth with his own.

They came apart reluctantly.

"Chrissy, I want you to know that you can trust me with your heart," he told her.

She could tell by his expression that he desperately wanted her to believe him. Aiden had no idea that it was

175

only a matter of time before he owned her heart.

Chapter 35

Jessica felt a sudden chill penetrate her body. She recognized the irritating shrill of Sabrina's voice coming toward her. She was seated in a chair dressed in a white robe with a cooling mint mask covering her face.

She had never known Sabrina to utilize spa services. Jessica peeked around the corner as much as she could.

She muttered a curse.

Sabrina was not alone. She was with Chrissy.

Jessica closed her eyes and took a deep cleansing breath. She had come to enjoy a day of pampering and two women that irritated her had chosen to interrupt her peaceful solitude.

A short time later, Chrissy and Sabrina strolled into the area where she sat. Jessica decided not to say anything to them. She hoped she could leave the room without them noticing her.

"I could've waxed my legs at home," Chrissy said. "Do you see the prices of this stuff?"

Sabrina laughed. "There is nothing wrong with a little pampering, girl. I see you're still tight with your money."

"It's called being wise."

Jessica bit back her laughter as she listened to them.

She had hoped they would discuss Natalia. She wanted some sign that her plan was progressing. Jessica had hoped that she would be in jail by this time. She wanted that last nail in her coffin already. Once Natalia was in prison, she could then expose Chrissy as a fraud. She would come to Traynor as Jessie Belle's daughter. She could claim that Reina knew of her existence. She would show him pictures of her father and his family. In fact, she had her features altered to look more like those of his sister. This time she would not be denied.

It was a good plan, but Jessica hated all this waiting, but Clayton convinced her that this was the best route to take if she wanted to connect to her family. If she'd done things the way she wanted—Chrissy and Natalia would already be dead. The last thing she needed was to leave a string of bodies behind.

Chapter 36

"Was it just me or did anyone have a weird vibe at the spa earlier?" Chrissy asked. "I don't know why, but it just didn't feel right."

Sabrina frowned. "In what way?"

"I can't explain it and I'm not paranoid, but I felt like Reina was there."

"Maybe it was because we have been talking about her a lot lately," Sabrina offered.

Chrissy shrugged. "It's probably all in my mind."

"Or maybe the lady that was in the room with us was really Reina."

They laughed.

"Okay, I have to prepare for my weekend with Aiden," Chrissy said. "I need to pick up a few things from the mall."

"If you wait until we close, I can go with you."

"That's fine."

"Don't take this the wrong way," Sabrina said, "but you should go to the spa more often. You look radiant."

"Maybe I will."

"Chrissy, I'm really happy for you. Look at all you've accomplished. And now, you have a man who loves you."

"I couldn't have done any of this without you and definitely not without God."

The telephone rang.

"Back to business," Sabrina murmured before answering the call.

⁂

Aiden glanced over at Chrissy and asked, "Have you ever eaten here?"

She nodded. "Once. I enjoyed the food."

Chrissy and Aiden had gotten up early to watch the sunrise. They arrived in Wilmington late last night. They sat up for almost three hours talking before calling it a night.

"You don't look overly excited about eating here. You've spent a lot of time here, so why don't you pick the restaurant?"

"Aiden, the food is good," she assured him. "This is the place you chose so we'll just eat lunch here."

"This isn't some sort of set-up, is it?"

Chrissy laughed. "C'mon."

She was mildly surprised that she hadn't noticed the soothing atmosphere of the restaurant, but maybe it was because she had dined outside on the sheltered patio during her last visit.

Aiden checked out the menu.

Chrissy and Aiden both chose the Caribbean empanada served over a bed of mixed greens.

When the food arrived, Chrissy waited for him to sample his meal.

"So what do you think?" she asked.

"It's not bad," Aiden answered. He sliced off another piece of his empanada and stuck a forkful into his mouth.

"I told you that the food was good."

"It's great," he responded.

After they left the restaurant, Chrissy and Aiden spent the rest of the afternoon shopping.

"When Chrissy walked out of the dressing room, he said, "I made dinner reservations for tonight."

"Where are we going?" She asked while eyeing her reflection in the mirror.

"It's a surprise."

"You should know that I'm not fond of surprises, Aiden."

"I'm sure you'll like this one."

While Aiden was next door in a sports shop, Chrissy purchased a watch he had been looking at from the jewelry door. She planned a little surprise of her own.

An hour later, they headed back to the house they'd rented for the weekend.

Chrissy stretched out on the sofa and Aiden sat down on the floor to watch a movie.

"I see why you like to come here. It's cathartic."

"I feel renewed after spending a few days at the beach. I've always loved the water."

After the movie, she said, "Why don't we just stay in

tonight. We can order take-out."

Aiden shook his head. "You're not getting off that easy."

Chrissy groaned as she rose to her feet. It was time to get ready.

She took a quick shower, then chose to wear a black maxi dress for their dinner.

Aiden was in the living room when she walked out of the bedroom. His eyes traveled from head to toe. "You look beautiful."

"You don't look too bad yourself," Chrissy responded with a grin.

He drove them to a nearby restaurant.

She frowned. "It looks crowded."

"We have reservations."

Inside, they were taken to a private dining room.

"What's all this?" Chrissy asked, looking around. "Are we the only ones eating in here?"

He nodded. "I didn't want to share you with the rest of the world—not tonight."

She kissed him on the lips. "You're such a sweetie."

Chrissy picked up the bouquet of roses. "You're spoiling me," she murmured.

"I know," Aiden said. "I know how much you love the yellow and red ones, but tonight I wanted you to have the sterling roses because they are a gift to the queen that you are." He took the flowers from her. "I have something else for you."

"What is that?" Chrissy asked, staring down at the gift-wrapped box.

"Open it."

She ripped off the wrapping and ribbon. Chrissy

couldn't contain her joy when she opened the box and saw the necklace. "You bought this for me. Oh, my goodness."

"I know how much you like crosses too. When I saw this one, I wanted to buy it for you," he said.

"This is so gorgeous," Chrissy murmured.

A waiter entered the room carrying a tray of food.

"We have crab cakes for starters and lobster bisque," Aiden said. "We are going to have wood grilled salmon for our entrée.

Chrissy smiled. "Everything sounds delicious."

"I hope it tastes good," he responded. "I made my choices based on recommendations by the chef."

She glanced around the room. "I can't believe you went through all this trouble for me. Aiden, this room is beautiful."

The staff had done a wonderful job with decorating the room. Tapered candles and floral arrangements all added to the romantic ambiance of the dining experience. Their table was draped in a rich, royal purple and gold theme and matched the multicolored curtains and carpet throughout.

Aiden pulled out a chair for Chrissy, and then sat down across from her.

"I can't put into words what I'm feeling right now," she said. "No one has ever done anything like this for me."

"I'm hoping that there will be more times like this. Chrissy, you should know by now that
I'm in love with you."

"Aiden, this is all so new to me, but I'm not afraid. I love you, too."

The arrival of the food placed a temporary hold on their conversation.

Chrissy tasted the salmon. "This is delicious."

Aiden agreed.

When they finished eating, Chrissy presented him with the gift she'd purchased for him. "I have a surprise for you."

Aiden opened the gift bag. "How did you know?"

"I saw you looking at the watches. The sales person told me that this is the one you were most interested in."

"I am a very lucky man to have someone like you in my life. There's something else I need to know, sweetheart. Do you love me enough to spend the rest of your life with me?" Aiden questioned.

His question caught her completely off guard. "Excuse me?"

Aiden flashed Chrissy a big grin. "Chrissy, I'm telling you that I want you to marry me. I love you and I want to wake up beside you every single morning."

"You want me to be your wife?" she asked, sounding surprised.

"Yes, I do. I'm not trying to rush you, but I want you to know my intentions." He pulled a tiny box out of his blazer. Opening it, he said, "I bought this for you as a promise ring. It's a one carat white sapphire that I had custom designed for you. I know that you're not into diamonds."

"This ring is gorgeous," she whispered. "Aiden, I absolutely love it."

After they prepared to leave, Chrissy wrapped her arms around him. "I'm so thankful you walked into my office that day. I never thought I'd come close to meeting a man like you, Aiden. I warn you, this is going to be so corny, but I have to say it. You are a dream come true."

"There is nothing corny about love."

Chapter 37

"Natalia, are you still spending time with Jessica?"

She glanced over at Chrissy. "Yes. Why did you ask me that?"

"Because I think she may not be who you think she is."

Natalia settled back in her chair. "What are you talking about?"

"All of this stuff came up after you met her and she's been to this house a few times. Suddenly, the police receive new information and they actually find it."

"And you think Jessica is behind this?"

"I think Reina is definitely behind the drama, but that Jessica is a pawn."

Natalia shook her head. "I don't think so, Chrissy. She has been nothing but a good friend."

"I hope you're right."

"Dean hasn't wanted me to say much, but we've been able to prove that the photos and the letter that was found here—they are fakes. The police don't want this information getting out because they are hoping that Reina will make a mistake."

"That's great. This lets you off the hook."

"I don't think they are entirely convinced that I'm innocent. Now please don't say anything about what I've just told you—not even to Sabrina."

"I won't" Chrissy promised.

"As for Jessica, I'll keep my eyes open to any red flags."

"Be careful, Natalia."

"Chrissy, I will. I'm not going to let Reina get away a second time."

"Well, I need to get back to the office. I was in the neighborhood showing a house and thought I'd drop by to check on you."

"Let's do lunch soon."

"I'll give you a call one-day next week."

Natalia watched Chrissy drive away before going back inside.

She thought about her relationship with Jessica. Could she be in cahoots with Reina? Natalia found it hard to believe, but it was possible.

When Dean arrived home that evening, she asked, "Hon, do you think Jessica could be involved with Reina?"

"Where did that come from?"

"Chrissy brought up the point that none of this stuff happened until after we met Jessica."

"It's probably a coincidence."

"Remember the night we had them over for dinner?

Didn't Clayton go to the bathroom?"

Dean sat down beside her. "Yeah. He's the only one who raised red flags for me, but I think we're looking in the wrong place. Jessica seems to really care about you."

Natalia's apprehension evaporated. Her husband had good instincts when it came to people and if he didn't believe Jessica was a fraud, then neither did she. "I feel like she's a good friend."

"I just left the police station and they are dropping the case for now."

"Really?"

"There's a lack of physical evidence and the D.A. is reluctant to move forward now. He believes that you were being framed."

Chapter 38

"She's been cleared," Jessica uttered. "Why didn't it work, Clayton? You said this plan was fool proof."

"I don't know what happened, but it's not over."

"I should've just killed her."

"And you'd be stuck in a prison somewhere. You allow your rage to take over, Jess. You don't think things out when you're caught up in your emotions. Look at you," he said, "You can't even be *you*."

Not in the mood to argue with Clayton, she stormed up the stairs.

Whirls of red swam before her. Jessica picked up one of the candlesticks on the mantle of the fireplace in the sitting room and flung it against a wall. *How could things have gone wrong?*

She opened the drawer of the nightstand on her side of the bed and pulled out a gun. Jessica could easily find out when Dean was going to be out of town. She would kill her then, she decided.

Jessica turned to find Clayton standing in the doorway. "You know that I'm crazy about you, Jess. Why don't you forget about those folks? I've always been here for you. I'm your family."

"I can't."

"You're the reason I came to Raleigh. You know how much I love New York, but I'm here for you."

"I appreciate everything you've done for me, Clayton." Jessica put the gun back in the drawer.

"Marry me, Jess."

She smiled. "You're sweet, but I'm too messed up to be anybody's wife."

He stroked her face. "You have been through a lot. I was too young to save you back then, but I promise I won't let anyone hurt you."

Staring off into space, she said, "Sometimes I feel that God took my son because He knew I wouldn't be a good mom."

"I don't believe that. We were young, but we would've been better parents than Gloria and Henry."

"Do you remember the night Gloria found out I was pregnant? Henry blamed you and lied saying that you had been sneaking in my room at night. Instead of denying it, you told Gloria that I was carrying your child."

Clayton uttered a curse. "We made them pay for their sins though."

She nodded. "Then we moved to New York."

"Why didn't you just stay with me, Jess?"

"Maybe if I had, things would've turned out differently."

"We're together now. I have enough money to last us five lifetimes. We can go back to New York and start our lives together as man and wife." He sat down beside her. "Babe, I have a bad feeling about this. I think it's time we left Raleigh."

"I can't leave just yet."

"Do you want to go to prison?" he snapped.

"Of course not."

"Then give up this vendetta, Jess."

She did not respond. Jessica was not about to make a promise that she didn't intend to keep.

Chapter 39

Holt walked up to Jessica's desk and said, "Do you have a few minutes?"

"Yes."

"I'd like to speak to you privately."

Jessica had no idea why Holt wanted to have a private conversation with her. Her guard went up as she rose to her feet. She followed him into his new office, closing the door behind her.

"Have I done something?" she asked.

Holt smiled. "Not at all. I plan on having one-on-ones with all of the staff."

Relaxed, she sat down in one of the visitor chairs, facing him.

"Mary Ellen was very fond of you."

"I enjoyed working with her as well, Holt."

"I'm hoping that you plan to stay on with the station."

Inside, Jessica was jumping for joy. She was thrilled with the opportunity to work with her brother. "Of course. I'll be happy to stay."

"I'm going to be working side by side with Holt," she told Clayton later that evening. "Everything is working out just like we planned."

"I'm glad you're getting what you want."

The terse tone of his voice caught Jessica's attention, prompting her to study his face. He looked as if he were trying to contain his temper. "Clayton, what's wrong?"

"I need to go to New York. One of my buildings was raided," he uttered. "Somebody had to talk…" He curled his hands into fists.

Jessica poured a glass of wine and brought it to him. "Can't that partner of yours take care of it?"

"He was picked up by the cops earlier."

"Then you need to stay as far away from New York right now," Jessica said. "What if he talks?"

"He won't."

"Clayton, what exactly happened?"

"That's what I'm going to New York to find out. All I know is that someone in my crew must've talked to the police."

"There's nothing that can link back to you, is there?"

"No. I've been very careful."

"When do you leave?"

"In a couple of hours," Clayton responded. "I should be back by the weekend."

"Are you going alone?"

"Yes."

There was no point in trying to change his mind. Jessica could tell from his body language that he was determined to seek out the threat to his organization. "Have you packed?"

He nodded toward the black leather duffel bag sitting near the door.

She noted he was wearing jeans—something Jessica hadn't seen on him in years. It was clear to her that he didn't want to draw attention to himself.

"I'll drive you to the airport."

"Miquel's taking me." Clayton walked over to her. "Babe, I'm sorry that I'm not in the best of moods right now. I just lost millions of dollars."

"I understand."

He kissed her. "I'm happy for you. You've worked hard to establish a relationship with Holt."

"Are you sure that going to New York right now is the best solution?"

"I don't like this any more than you do, but I don't see any other choice."

"Are you sure this is not some sort of set-up? Maybe this is what they *want* you to do—to catch the big fish."

Clayton seemed to be considering her words. "I hadn't thought of that."

"I think you should wait this out a few days. Show up when no one is expecting you or better yet, let Nikko or Miguel get on the plane tonight. They can check things out for you."

Chapter 40

Natalia pressed her hand to her stomach as she eyed her reflection in the mirror. She was going to have a baby. The doctor confirmed it earlier at her appointment. She could hardly wait for Dean to return. He was going to be so excited.

The way she was feeling right now—nothing could put a damper on her mood, not even Reina. Since her name had been cleared, Natalia feared that she would show up on her doorstep ready to finish what she started, but to her relief, there had been no signs of her.

Natalia decided to put aside her worries to rejoice over the news that she was pregnant. She would be a mother in over seven and a half months. She didn't care if it was a boy or girl, as long as her baby was healthy.

Jessica was coming over to have dinner with her. She was grateful for the company. Natalia thought about Chrissy's suspicions. Thank God she was wrong about Jessica. She had come to value her as a friend. Natalia normally did not get along with women in general, but she and Jessica had found common ground.

However, there were times when she thought she glimpsed a coldness in Jessica's eyes, but Natalia was sure it was her imagination.

The doorbell sounded.

"Jessica, I'm glad you're here. Dinner is almost ready."

"Thank you for inviting me."

"You know how I hate eating alone," Natalia said as they settled down in the family room. "I normally don't cook when Dean's away. I just grab a sandwich or a salad."

Jessica grinned. "I feel honored."

"I invited my cousin and Sabrina, but they both had other plans for tonight."

"Oh. That's too bad."

"I really want you all to get to know one another."

"I'm sure we will when the time is right."

Natalia nodded in agreement. "Well, it's just you and me. Let's make it a night to remember."

Chapter 41

Jessica was thrilled when she found out Chrissy and Sabrina would not be coming because she wanted Natalia alone. The twit had no idea that she was in the last hours of her life.

She had parked her rental down the street. Jessica was dressed in black from head to toe. Her cap obscured her features so that anyone watching could not describe her face. She decided a gun would be too noisy so she decided to steal some of the vials Clayton kept in the safe and a syringe.

"You look cute in that hat," Natalia said. "This is a different look for you."

"I'm trying something new."

She poured Jessica a glass of wine.

"Aren't you drinking any," Jessica asked.

Jacquelin Thomas

"No," Natalia responded. "I won't be drinking any wine for a while."

Comprehension dawned. "Are you pregnant?"

"Yes. Dean doesn't know yet, but I had to share this with someone. I'm so excited."

A baby. Natalia was pregnant.

As much as Jessica hated Natalia, she could not bring herself to harm the child she carried. Now she had to rethink everything. She hated herself for months following Charlottes demise. She hated leaving Leah without her mother.

"Jessica, are you okay?" Natalia inquired.

"I'm fine. I was just thinking how fortunate you are to have a baby. They are blessings from God."

"I'm so sorry about your son."

Jessica shrugged. "It just wasn't meant to be."

"When you and Clayton get married, you are planning to try again?"

"Natalia, I'm not as young as you, sweetie. We have been thinking about adoption though."

"I think that's wonderful."

"There are so many children who need a home and need to be loved."

"You sound as if you know what that feels like."

Jessica lifted her gaze to meet Natalia's. "I can relate in some ways, but I love children… I wanted a house full, but we don't always get what we want."

"You have a heart full of love to give. You'd be a wonderful mother."

Jessica left Natalia's house shortly after nine p.m.

When she arrived home, Clayton was waiting for her. "You went into the safe."

She handed him the vials and the syringe. "It's all there."

"Why did you change your mind?"

"Natalia's pregnant."

Jessica dropped down on the bed. "I'm tired, Clayton. I'm tired of being angry… I'm just tired."

"Then let it go."

Her eyes filled with water. "Traynor's getting married in a couple of weeks. Everyone will be there except me. I am a part of his family and I won't be able to celebrate with them. It's not right, Clayton. I didn't do anything to deserve the life I was given."

"I saw the announcement in the newspaper," Clayton said. "The very thing you want is right here in front of you. I am your family, Jess. I have always been your family."

"I just wish it were enough," she whispered.

Chapter 42

Traynor and Angela were pronounced man and wife in a small ceremony at Traynor's house. It pleased Chrissy to see him happy and hopeful for the future. Although she hadn't known him very long, he seemed nothing like the man she had heard about—it was as if he had become numb.

As his courtship with Angela progressed, Chrissy started to see life in Traynor once more. Her eyes traveled to Holt. He appeared happy for his father.

Angela looked elegant in her ivory and silver suit. Chrissy felt she was a good match for Traynor. She was intelligent and powerful in her own right, but she seemed content to stand beside her new husband without being in the limelight.

In lieu of a fancy reception dinner, the couple opted for

low country boil held in the backyard of Traynor's house. It was Angela's idea to serve the dish of shrimp, corn, sausage and vegetables in honor of their southern roots.

"Congratulations Traynor. I'm very happy for you." Chrissy embraced him.

"Thank you for coming to celebrate with us."

"I thought you might be bringing a guest with you."

She grinned. "Now why would you think that?"

"Since I've seen that light in your eyes. I figured only one thing could put it there—blooming love."

"I always knew you were a romantic."

"I guess I am."

"I didn't bring him because it's still new. I'm not rushing into anything. I don't want to give him the wrong idea. Besides, I haven't told him about our relationship."

"Real love is unconditional and nonjudgmental, Chrissy."

Traynor left a few minutes later to join his bride.

Chrissy joined Holt at the table. "Where is Franke and the kids?"

"Upstairs in the playroom. She's trying to get them down for a nap."

"The ceremony was beautiful, even without all the fluff and flair."

Her brother agreed. "I haven't seen Dad this happy in a long time."

"So you're really okay with this marriage?"

"Yes. Dad loved our mother with his entire being. He stuck by her even when she didn't deserve it—there were no shadows across his heart when she died. Dad deserves to find love again."

"Despite her faults, Jessie Belle raised an amazing son."

"And she missed out on getting to know her wonderful daughter."

Chrissy broke into a smile. "Thank you for saying that."

"You're not going to get all emotional on me now."

"Of course not. I've never been that kind of girl. Your sister is a boss chick."

"How is your new assistant working out?"

"Holt, you were right. Laura is great."

"I'm glad to hear that. She gave her testimony on Sunday. She is so thankful for having that job."

"I'm blessed to have her. She is very organized and keeps me on track."

Chrissy left for home two hours later.

"Hey beautiful," Aiden said when she answered the phone. "Are you in the mood for company?"

"I just got home, but give me an hour."

"Have you eaten?"

"Don't worry about getting food. I know you love seafood. I have a nice big plate of low country boil."

"I knew you were the girl for me."

She laughed. "I'll see you in an hour, silly."

Chapter 43

Jessica seethed in anger when she spotted Chrissy leaving Traynor's house. *I should have been there. Holt is my brother which makes me family.* How could they believe that whore was a part of their family? *I ought to just walk up in there and announce that the prodigal daughter has returned home.*

The more she thought about it, her need to be accepted increased. Jessica opened her door and stepped out of the Mercedes.

She was almost near the house when reality sank in. She couldn't just blow her cover like this. Clayton was right—she couldn't let her emotions take over.

Jessica turned and headed back to the car. It was not the time for a family reunion.

Chapter 44

"Hi Jessica."

She looked up, surprised to see Chrissy standing there. "Hey, how are you?"

"I'm fine."

"Are you here to see Holt?"

"I am," she confirmed. "We have a lunch date."

"I wasn't aware that you and Holt knew each other."

Chrissy gave a tiny smile. "He's my brother."

Jessica sat back in her chair. "It's a small world ..."

"Yes, it is."

The telephone rang.

"Excuse me," Jessica said.

Chrissy observed her as she jotted down notes during her call. She was drawn to Jessica's handwriting. There was something very familiar about it.

When Jessica looked up, she pretended to be looking

at her phone.

"I'm sorry about that."

"Oh no, you're at work. I understand." Chrissy picked up a bridal magazine. "Congratulations on your upcoming wedding."

Jessica smiled. "Thank you. Clayton and I are very excited." She pushed away from her desk. "Holt is upstairs. I'll go get him."

"Thank you."

As soon as Jessica disappeared, Chrissy took pictures of the note and of her signature, then put her phone away.

She was seated with a magazine when Jessica returned with Holt.

"Jessica, it was good seeing you," Chrissy said as they headed toward the exit doors.

In the car, she told Holt, "I know you're going to think I'm crazy, but I'm not."

"What's going on, Chris?"

"I noticed something about Jessica's handwriting. It's very similar to Reina's."

"How would you know that?"

"I have her journal," she said. "I've studied it so much that I'd recognize her writing style anywhere. It's the way she makes her J's."

"If what you're saying is true…" Holt didn't finish the thought. "Dear Lord…"

"She's been right under our nose all this time."

He shook his head. "I can't believe it."

"She had to have work done on her face and wearing contacts, but I believe that it's her. It's the only way she could come back here and move around unnoticed. Then there's her fiancé, Clayton. The person who purchased the salons was named Clayton Wallace. I'm pretty sure they are the same person."

"This is crazy," Holt uttered.

"Truth is often stranger than fiction. I heard that somewhere and I think it applies in this situation."

"What should we do now?"

"Nothing yet. We don't want to spook her. Holt, when you go back to the station, please don't say anything. Just act normal."

"I'm calling Dad. Let's get together tonight at my house. We can try to come up with a solution as a family."

❧

"Here are the pictures of her handwriting earlier," Chrissy began, "and this is from the journal."

"They match," Traynor said after looking at them. "Reina and Jessica are the same person."

Angela compared the photos next. "She has a very distinct way that she makes her 'J's."

"One of the guests commented how close Jessica's name was to Mom's." Holt said. "I thought he was just talking about her first name, but he was referring to both her first and last name."

"She has a Spanish surname," Chrissy interjected. "Campana…"

"Which is *Bell* when translated to English," Angela stated.

"Jessica Bell," Chrissy uttered.

"I wanted to be sure it wasn't some weird coincidence so after lunch, I did a records search and could not find anything past the last year." Holt sat down beside his wife.

"This is unbelievable," Frankie said.

"If it wasn't Reina we're talking about, I would probably feel the same way." Chrissy folded her arms across her chest. "The thing is what do we do about this?"

"Call the police," Traynor interjected.

"No."

"Why not, Chrissy?" Angela questioned. "From everything I've heard—that woman is dangerous."

"I want a chance to talk to her first. She is my sister and I feel that out of all of us—I understand her pain and anger. Reina needs help."

"You'd be putting yourself in danger," Holt said.

"Do you think she had anything to do with Mary Ellen's death?" Frankie blurted. "She was fine until Reina started working with her."

Traynor shook his head. "I don't think she could've done something like that—the police are convinced by the toxicology reports that it was just a tragic accident. The stuff in the aquarium was toxic and it entered her system through a couple of paper cuts. I don't believe Reina could've engineered her death."

"I'm going to set up a meeting with her," Chrissy announced. "Maybe I can talk her into turning herself in. I'll even go to the police station with her."

"She won't do it," Holt said. "I tried to get her to do it before she ran off. Chrissy, I know you want to help Reina—we all do, but she might hurt you."

Chrissy gazed at her brother. "You don't have to worry about me. I can take care of myself."

"I still think you should call the police."

"Oh, I plan to call them, Frankie. Especially if she won't go willingly."

Chapter 45

"Hello Reina," Chrissy said when Jessica answered the phone.

"Excuse me?"

"I know it's you. We need to talk."

Her words were met with silence.

"Look, this is just between you and me. No police."

"I'm sorry but I have no idea what you're talking about. You obviously have the wrong person."

"Don't do this. All I want to do is talk. We have a lot to talk about, don't you think?"

"We just might have something to discuss. Like your infiltration into the Deveraux family. I'd love to hear how you accomplished that."

"Good," Chrissy responded. "Why don't we get together around seven? I can come to you if you'd like."

"I'll give you a call when I'm ready to have that conversation and I'll pick the location."

"You have twenty-four hours."

Chrissy hung up the phone. "The ball is in your court, sister dear."

Chapter 46

Jessica muttered a curse.

She was not about to let her guard down where Chrissy was concerned. How did she know? Did Holt know as well? Jessica decided it was time for her to leave the office permanently. She grabbed her purse and headed to her car.

As soon as she reached the house, she called Clayton. "I just got a call from Chrissy. She knows."

"Jess, don't you do anything until I get back to Raleigh. I'll take care of everything. In fact, why don't you fly to New York tonight?"

"I'm not leaving just yet," she responded. "She says that she wants to talk—so we're going to have a conversation."

"She may be trying to set you up."

"She won't see me coming, babe."

"I'm serious, Jess," Clayton said. "This just doesn't feel right to me. Wait until I get home."

Jessica paced, her heels tapping a steady rhythm across the marble floor. *I am not about to let that little twit think she's in control.* She picked up a pillow and tossed it across the room. Chrissy may have Traynor and Holt fooled, but not her. Jessica was going to expose the imposter, and then destroy her.

Clayton wanted her to wait, but Jessica could not. She had to strike quickly.

With renewed purpose, she rushed upstairs and changed into all black.

Gloves on, Jessica pulled a vial and syringe from a leather case in her closet and slipped it into her jacket.

She had the element of surprise on her side. This way Chrissy wouldn't be able to alert anyone, especially the police.

Chapter 47

Chrissy entered her apartment and sat her purse on the decorative chest near the door. She stood in place, overcome by an innate sense of danger. Every nerve in her body strained on alert for the smallest sound or slightest movement, she glanced around. "You might as well come on out. I know you're here."

Jessica strolled out of the master bedroom. "Hello sis..."

"I actually liked the way you looked before," Chrissy said, and then added, "Reina, you are so predictable. I knew you'd try something like this."

"Then what comes next shouldn't be a surprise to you," Jessica stated.

Chrissy smiled. "Surely you don't think that I was not prepared for this little visit."

Jessica laughed. "Am I supposed to be scared now?"

"Why did you come back to Raleigh? Why didn't you just stay away?"

"I have unfinished business here."

"Are you referring to me?" Chrissy questioned.

Jessica asked a question of her own. "How did you do it? How did you convince Traynor and Holt that you were Jessie Belle's daughter?"

"It's the truth. I have a DNA test to prove it. Jessie Belle gave birth to two girls that night. Gloria kept you but she dropped me off at a hospital. Apparently, I was born with a few problems."

"No, I didn't know about you. I thought I was Jessie Belle's only daughter." Jessica shrugged. "She really was something else."

"Yes, she was… but she isn't the only one. You've made quite a name for yourself, Rei… Jessica… whatever your name is…"

"It's really Jessica. You have her face and I was left with a form of her name. Jessica Belle Ricks." She gave a short laugh. "How ironic is that?"

"Just so you know… she rejected me, too."

Her eyes narrowing, Jessica asked, "She knew about you?"

"I confronted her after I had the DNA test run," Chrissy said. "Jessie Belle didn't care about the truth. She wanted nothing to do with a whore. Her words."

Jessica frowned. "She actually said that to you?"

Chrissy nodded.

"We didn't fit into her perfect little family, I guess." Jessica paused a moment before saying, "But you found your way in…"

"Traynor found Jessie Belle's journals, and he figured out that she had twins. He wanted Holt to get to know his sisters. They care about you, too."

"Don't lie to me."

"I'm not," Chrissy said. "We all care about you."

Jessica shook her head. "I'm not stupid."

"I know that. You and I… Jessica, we were dealt a bad hand in life. Traynor and Holt both understand. They don't want to dwell in the past."

"I hurt people…"

"You *killed* people, Jessica." She pulled a small gun out of her pocket and pointed it at her sister. "Which is why I am going to get you some help."

"Nice move. I have to admit I wasn't expecting this turn of events."

Chrissy eyes never left Jessica's face as she pressed a number on her security keypad and said, "Send the police. I have an intruder in my home. I'm armed. I have a gun on the intruder."

Jessica looked as if she wanted to approach her.

She cocked the trigger. "Don't try it. I know how to use this gun and I'm a very good shot."

"And here I thought we were bonding."

"We will have plenty of time to bond when you're behind bars."

"So this is your end game. You want Holt and Traynor all to yourself," Jessica accused.

"That's not it at all," Chrissy said. "Believe it or not, I want you to get psychiatric help. I know what it's like to go down that dark road. Sometimes you need some assistance to get back."

"I'm not crazy."

"No, you're not," Chrissy agreed. "You're broken though. I know because I was the same way not too long ago."

She heard police sirens in the distance.

"You're really going to do this?"

"Yes," Chrissy responded. "I'm pretty sure you are the one responsible for what's been going on with Natalia. I can't let you hurt anyone else."

Jessica took a step forward.

"I'll shoot you," Chrissy warned, "*I mean it.*"

"You are no better than me."

"Exactly. That's why I have no problem pulling the trigger." Her gun still trained on

Jessica, she inched backwards to unlock the front door.

"In here," Chrissy called out. "The door isn't locked."

Jessica smiled. "Another time... another day..."

Two policemen burst into the apartment, guns drawn.

"I called you," Chrissy said. "This is my place. Be careful, she may have a needle or something,"

"Hands up in the air," One of the officers yelled.

Jessica did as she was instructed.

The officer walked over and immediately handcuffed her.

"Do you know her?" the other officer asked.

"Yes," Chrissy responded, "She's my sister."

⁂

"You did the right thing, Chrissy."

She looked up at Traynor. "I feel horrible for turning her over to the police like that."

"You had no other choice," Frankie interjected. "Although they didn't find anything on her, I'm sure she came to harm you."

"I don't think so." Chrissy touched her forehead. "She wants a family. She didn't do anything to you and Holt the last time. I don't believe she would've hurt me."

Frankie glanced over at Traynor. "Do you think she had anything to do with Mary Ellen's death?"

He shook his head. "Her death was ruled as accidental. There's no way that Jessica could know just how toxic the reef or whatever it's called in Mary Ellen's aquarium. I think it was a coincidence."

"Chris, how much do you know about her life?" Holt inquired.

"I read her journal—she had to deal with physical and verbal abuse. On top of that, she was molested repeatedly by Gloria's husband and ended conceiving a child with him when she was only fourteen. Her son was stillborn... can you believe that Gloria actually blamed Jessica?"

Traynor sat down beside his wife on the loveseat. "She's got a lot of anger built up."

"She has enough reasons to be angry," Holt responded. "Dealing with all that would mess anybody up."

"I know that Jessica has done some terrible things, but the parental maltreatment she experienced had a huge influence on the person she's become," Angela said. "Just from what I've heard, she probably has borderline personality disorder."

"Why do you say that?" Chrissy asked.

"Studies of people diagnosed with BPD have a high prevalence of childhood sexual abuse. It's been estimated that seventy-five percent of people with this disorder have a history of childhood sexual abuse. Physical and emotional abuse are all associated with the development of BPD. For some, the disorder is a defense mechanism against the childhood trauma."

"I can understand that," Chrissy said. "But how likely is it that she and I both have mental disorders?"

"I'm no expert in genetics," Angela responded, "but given what you both have gone through—it's very possible."

Chrissy wanted to call Aiden, but she did not. He had no knowledge of her relationship with Traynor and Holt, or anything about Jessica. He was out of town on business, but would be back at the end of the week. She decided that when he returned, she would tell him as soon as he returned.

Chapter 48

I should've listened to Clayton. If I'd gone to New York like he requested, I wouldn't be here in this horrid place.

Jessica kept her eyes trained on the two rows of shower heads painted in rust. She counted twenty in all.

"Strip down," a female guard ordered.

Her lips turned downward as she slowly observed her dismal surroundings—chipped tile that was once white, covered the walls and floor of the room. The fluorescent lights cast a yellowing shadow, adding to the ugliness and misery.

"*Strip.* I'm not gon' tell you again."

Her warning did not faze Jessica. She had survived worse and she would not let this break her. She came in with a name, but would eventually become only a number in the prison system. She would not be like the other women in jail with their faces worn and defeat in their spirits.

Jessica stared the guard in the face as she removed her shirt and jeans. She lifted her chin defiantly before taking off her thong panties and matching bra.

"No shower shoes?" she asked. "This place smells of mold and disease."

"Honey, this ain't no spa."

Quickly, Jessica stepped under the shower head, braving the stinging spray of hot water. Just as she began to lose herself in the water, it was suddenly turned off.

She was given a small white towel that felt like sandpaper on her skin. Jessica quickly noted that her clothes were gone, a gray jumpsuit, too-big panties, and a white tee-shirt in their place. Without a word, she put them on.

Jessica was lead down a hall to a section of cells with cots. She slid her eyes toward them. Some were occupied—women silently watching as she walked past.

"Here."

She stared at the metal-framed bed and worn mattress. Jessica was horrified at the stained toilet and sink. The small room was so cold and awful that she shivered.

"Make your bed up," the guard said before stepping out of the cell.

The door closed.

Jessica swallowed a sob as she spread her dingy white sheet on the thin mattress, then covered it with a navy blanket.

She sat numb on the edge of the cot, listening.

The sound of footsteps reverberated through the cell block. Jessica could hear someone crying. She could hear another woman screaming and cussing.

This was just a jailhouse—it was not her final destination, but as much as Jessica fought it, she was afraid of what was to come.

She willed herself to stand up and walk over to the door.

Metal.

She would spend the rest of her life in a room similar to this. Strangely, Jessica never once considered that she would end up in jail—in a small, cramped place. Her heart beat wildly.

Unable to hold back her tears, Jessica snatched the rough blanket off the bed as she sank to the floor sobbing.

❧

"Move ahead, Ricks." The guard put her hand on Jessica's shoulder and gave her a light shove.

Jessica's face tightened in anger but she did not respond. Her eyes traveled to where her visitor sat.

"So here we are..." she murmured when she picked up the receiver on her side of the partition.

"I really hate that it has to be with you behind bullet-proof glass," Chrissy uttered.

"You're the one who put me here."

"It was for your own good, Jessica."

She raised her eyes without lifting her head. "I don't happen to agree."

"We were both abandoned by Jessie Belle." Chrissy leaned forward. "It deeply affected us both."

Jessica chuckled. "Abandonment issues? Is that why I'm the way I am?"

"I think so. I really believe that it's a huge part of the

problem."

Her eyes narrowed. "Why are *you* here, Chrissy? You don't like me and I care even less about you."

"I came because you're my sister and I want to help you."

"Right… I'm supposed to believe that you had me put in jail just so that you could help me. Help me how? To a lethal injection?"

"You are in jail for the crimes you committed, plain and simple. The truth is that Traynor and Holt care a great deal about you… so do I. This is why I'm here now." Chrissy took a deep breath. "You need help, Jessica. You're mentally ill."

Her lids raised half way in an expression that was weary and guarded. "I'm fine."

"Traynor's talked to a lawyer and there's a good chance the courts will give you a reduced sentence because of the mental illness, but you're going to have to agree to get the help you need, Jessica."

"I think I'll just wait for a doctor to tell me if there's something wrong with me. I'm just another angry black woman, as far as I'm concerned."

Chrissy shook her head. "It runs much deeper than that."

"When did you become such an expert? Oh, one of your Johns must have been a psychiatrist."

"Actually, it was one of my *customers* that indicated that I might be bipolar. He referred me to someone. Turns out, he was right."

"Just because we're twins does not mean that I'm bipolar."

"I don't think you're bipolar," Chrissy stated. "There's

something more going on with you."

Jessica laughed.

"There is still hope for you. I know because I was in a dark place like you, but with therapy and my relationship with the Lord… I can better manage my manic episodes. I am praying that one day they will eventually stop."

"Even if I believed you, my life is not worth fighting for, Chrissy. I overplayed my hand and now I'm here."

"Do you have an ounce of regret for what you've done?" When Jessica did not respond, Chrissy pushed on. "I know that you're filled with rage, but deep down, I know that you have a heart and a conscience."

Jessica wasn't playing her sister's game. "You can't save me and I certainly don't need your pity. If you're trying to get more crowns in Heaven… you're out of luck."

"I never figured you for a quitter."

"You don't know anything about me."

"I know more than you think," Chrissy responded. "I have your journal."

"Did you read it?"

"Yeah, I did."

Jessica muttered a curse.

"With all that you endured, I can understand why you have psychotic episodes, but you can still live a life that's worth fighting for, Jessica. This battle is still yours to win."

She shrugged. "Not interested."

Chrissy's expression changed, the hope drained away as the light in her eyes dimmed. She was disappointed.

"I thought you would be here to gloat."

"I don't like seeing you like this. Family means a lot to the both of us. I wanted it so badly that I confronted Jessie Belle the night she fell."

"You were *there*?"

Chrissy nodded.

Jessica shifted in her chair. She sat up straight, suddenly engaged. "It was *you*."

"I was so angry and in a manic state... it's no excuse and it's something I have to live with for the rest of my life."

"Does Traynor know about this?"

"Yes, I told him the night you ran off."

"Yet, they welcomed you into the family."

"They will do the same with you, Jessie. They want to help you."

"Then why am I sitting on this side?"

"Because you're a danger to others," Chrissy responded, "but it won't always be this way."

"I'm not stupid. This is what all of you wanted—me behind bars. Now you all can go off and be a family."

Chrissy shook her head. "Our family will never be whole without you, Jessica."

"Time's up," The guard announced.

"Do me a favor and don't come back here," Jessica stated.

Back in her cell, she sat on the edge of her cot with tears running down her face.

Chapter 49

"I am so glad that psycho is locked behind bars," Natalia stated as she settled down on the sofa beside her cousin. "I allowed Jessica in my life and the whole time she was trying to set me up to go to prison. She had all that plastic surgery to come back to Raleigh and ruin lives... who in their right mind would do that?"

"The person you're referring to is Chrissy's twin, so can you be just a tad bit sympathetic?" Sabrina asked.

"Sorry, but she is one dangerous woman."

Chrissy did not respond.

"She must have had a huge laugh at my expense." Natalia shook her head. "I should have listened to you, Chrissy. You tried to warn me."

"I thought she might be connected to Reina—I didn't know they were the same person."

"She probably would've tried to hurt me if I hadn't been pregnant."

Chrissy looked at her. "Why do you say that?"

"It was the look she gave me when she found out I was having a baby. It didn't make sense to me then, but now that I think about it—she didn't want to hurt my child." Natalia took a sip of her tea. "I guess she does have a heart after all."

"I'm going to see Jessica," Chrissy announced.

"What for?" Sabrina and Natalia asked in unison.

"I need to talk to her."

"What is it about that psycho?" Natalia demanded. "You *do* realize that she went to your house to kill you."

"She is my sister."

"I know you are hoping for a happy ending, Chrissy, but it's just not going to happen."

"Natalia…" Sabrina said. "Don't…"

"No. She needs to know what she's dealing with," Natalia insisted. "Jessica is crazy."

"I know that she hurt you," Chrissy responded.

"She did more than hurt me. Jessica tried to make it look as if I killed Mike and Charlotte. Those pictures and that letter could've ruined my marriage."

"You have to understand that she's not well. Besides, we've all done things that we regret."

"I don't think she regrets anything, which is even more reason that you need to just let them bury her under the jail," Natalia said.

"Jessica has a mental illness and I intend to see that she gets the help she needs."

"Being bipolar is one thing, but your sister is a murderer."

"Natalia, I'm not going to abandon her. She's been through enough. Everything that's happened to her is what started her on this road in the first place."

"You read her journal?"

Chrissy nodded. "Traynor gave it to me along with Jessie Belle's journals."

"It's still no excuse for the crimes she's committed." Natalia folded her arms across her chest. "I can't tell you what to do, but I will say that you're wasting your time with that one."

"I don't agree. I believe that I can reach her."

"What you need to do is walk away and leave her locked up where she can't hurt anybody."

"Natalia, I'm not going to give up on Jessica. I can't do it."

Chapter 50

Jessica silently debated whether to talk to Chrissy. Curiosity got the better of her, so she told the guard, "I want to see my visitor."

"I thought you said you didn't want to see anyone."

"I changed my mind."

She followed the guard to the visitor station.

Chrissy was already seated.

"What are you doing here?" she asked as soon as she picked up the receiver.

"Jessica, I told you that I would never abandon you. I meant what I said."

"When did you become so forgiving?"

"When I realized the magnitude of God's love for us. He sent His son to the world to die for our sins."

"Do you really think that God still loves someone like me?"

Chrissy nodded. "Of course."

Jessica chuckled. "I'm beginning to think you're the one who is crazy. If God loved me—he never would've put me through the hell I had to live with. Something broke inside me a long time ago, Chrissy. I can't be fixed."

"I don't believe that. My life wasn't anything to brag about either, but I survived and I'm better now. I have to take medication, but it's okay. I'm not defined by the bad things I've done or the fact that I'm bipolar. I also have faith in divine healing."

"So now you're a former prostitute turned super saint, huh?"

"I'm not a saint by any means, Jessica. I'm still flawed, but I know that as long as I have breath in my body—I have another chance to get it right."

"Good for you."

"Your life isn't over."

"Yet," Jessica uttered. "I could get a life sentence or the death penalty."

"I don't believe that's going to happen," Chrissy said, "God's not done with you."

She gave a short laugh. "You've been saved a hot minute and now you have a hotline to God."

"There is someone else who would like to see you, Jessica."

"Who?"

"Your brother," Chrissy announced. "Holt is here."

Jessica's eyes watered. "I don't believe you."

"He's right outside. I'm going to leave so that the two of you can talk."

"Jessica... how are you?" Holt inquired.

"I know that you really could care less, so I won't bother answering that question. I'd like to know why you are here—is it to gloat?"

He shook his head. "I am here because you are my sister. I want you to know that I forgive you for all that you've done."

"How can you?"

"Because God requires it of me."

"Okay, your conscience is clear," Jessica responded, "You can leave now."

"Despite all you've done, I am not going to abandon you."

She gave a short laugh. "I guess it's easy for you to say that because I'm most likely going to prison for the rest of my life."

"Jessica, I have to confess that there was a time when I wanted nothing more for you, but now I only want you to get the help that you need."

"It's really hard to believe that you and I came from the same mother. Jessie Belle wouldn't have cared as long as I didn't interfere in her life."

"She wasn't perfect, but I love and forgave her," Holt stated. "You are my sister and I will not let you go through this alone."

"I don't need you, Holt."

"That's what you've come to expect, isn't it?"

"What are you talking about?"

"You expect people to just walk out of your life. You want people to believe that it doesn't matter, but deep down... you're so angry with the world that you can't see straight."

"What are you? My Shrink? You and Chrissy missed your calling."

"I'm your brother," he responded softly. "We got you an attorney."

"I can get my own lawyer."

"Jessica, we want to help you. Whether you want to admit it—you need help and I'm not sure you will find it in prison."

"Oh, I get it. You think I should be in an institution."

"Not really," Holt said, "I do think that you need to be in a place where you will get the medication and counseling that you need."

"I've done some horrible things."

"I know."

"You should be afraid of me."

"I'm not," he said. "I do not believe you'd ever harm me because we're family."

"North Carolina is a death penalty state. I'm sure I'm headed to death row, Holt. I'd prefer if we said our final goodbyes now."

"You will come to see that I'm just as stubborn as you are."

A smile tugged at her lips. "You know this is really ironic. All my life, I've wanted nothing more than family. It is because of that desire that I'm sitting on this side of the jail."

"Will you please let Angela represent you? She will do everything she can to keep you off death row."

"If I agree, will you and Chrissy stay away?"

He looked into her eyes and said, "No. We are both committed to supporting you throughout this ordeal."

Holt watched as Jessica got up and followed the guard

back to her cell.

For the first time in my life, I'm scared.

She wiped away a lone tear. There was a small part of her being that wanted to trust Chrissy and Holt.

⁊₭

"Hello daughter."

Jessica sat up on the uncomfortable cot. "Jessie Belle?"

"You've been a very bad girl, haven't you?"

She wiped her eyes. "What? How can you be here?"

"There are people that care about you. They want to help you, so let them."

"The only person I really wanted to care about me was you."

"I know." Jessie Belle moved to sit on the edge of the cot. "I made some terrible mistakes and I'm not proud of it. One of those mistakes was how I treated you and Chrissy. I wanted to take it all back, but I couldn't. I'd dug a hole for myself that I couldn't climb out of."

"So have I," Jessica murmured.

"The difference is that you still have life. You still have a chance to turn things around for yourself."

"I never wanted your money or anything—I just wanted to be a part of your family."

"I realized it, but it was already too late. I hope that one day you will be able to forgive me."

Jessica did not respond.

"The hurt you feel is too great, but maybe in time."

"Maybe ... "

"You are no longer alone," Jessie Belle said as she placed a hand to Jessica's cheek.

Jessica woke up with a start.

Shaken, she glanced around her tiny cell. It had been a dream. However, Jessie Belle's perfume still lingered in the air, and her cheek was still warm from her mother's touch.

❦

Clayton visited her the next day.

"You know how much I hate being anywhere near a jail," he uttered. "Why didn't you listen to me?"

"I should have," Jessica responded. "I'm really sorry."

"We had everything, babe."

"I'm not good for you, Clayton."

"I don't ever want to hear you say something like that again. My lawyer has agreed to take your case. I—"

"I already have an attorney," she interjected. "Angela Saxon-Deveraux is going to represent me."

His eyes narrowed. "What are you doing, Jess?"

Holt and Chrissy both feel that she can really help me. I meet with her tomorrow." Jessica decided not to mention her conversation with Jessie Belle—he would surely think she was losing her mind.

"They've been here to see you?"

"Yes. I'm just as surprised as you are. They think that I'm mentally ill and they want to help me."

"How do you feel about this?"

Jessica shrugged. "Who doesn't have a little crazy inside them?"

"This may actually work in your favor," he said as he stroked his chin. "If they want you to see a psychiatrist—do it."

"I am. Maybe he or she can tell me why I'm so angry

all of the time."

"You've been through a lot, babe. Make sure you don't leave anything out when you talk with that psychiatrist."

Their gazes met and held.

"You think there's something wrong with me, too."

"Not anything that's your fault," Clayton admitted. "I love you, Jess. Nothing will ever change that."

Chapter 51

"Hello Jessica."

"Angela…" She paused a moment before saying, "Thank you for representing me. I have to tell you that I don't have much hope in the legal system."

"I'm going to talk to the district attorney to see if we can work out a plea deal so that you won't have to go to court. But first, I'd like you to speak with a psychologist."

Jessica shrugged. "Sure…whatever."

"We are all concerned about you."

"Why do you care? You don't even know me."

"I know many women like you and I don't believe that your being in prison for the rest of your life will do you any good."

"So the plan is for me to spend my life in a mental hospital? Either way, I'm locked away from the world."

"Don't give up now, Jessica. You've always been a fighter."

"For five days, I got up when I was told, went to bed when I was told, ate when and what I was told … I have to wear this ugly jumpsuit, sleep on a cot and use toilet paper that leaves scratches on my behind. It's finally sunk in that this is my life. It's my truth." Jessica wiped away a tear that escaped her left eye. "I don't want to die," she whispered. "After everything I've done… I fear dying."

"I'm going to do everything I can to make sure you don't."

"Are you doing this to impress Traynor?"

Angela shook her head. "I wanted to represent you because I want to help you. I don't think you belong in a prison facility with overworked doctors who prescribe electroshock and medication that will keep you so drugged you won't even know what's going on. My daughter was diagnosed with a mental illness. It was so severe that she ran away with a pervert she'd met on the Internet. She ended up killing him during a manic state. She went to prison."

"You were married to Congressman Will Saxon. I remember you now. You and your late husband shared this story during the campaign."

Angela nodded. "The prison my daughter was in, was underfunded and understaffed. They employed part-time doctors who didn't fully understand the complexity of my daughter's illness… and she wasn't the only inmate in this situation."

"Your daughter committed suicide."

"Yes. When she died, my husband and I vowed that we would fight for people like her. People with a mental illness used to be treated in hospitals, but now we're punishing behaviors that we once tried to treat."

"Do you really think I'm crazy?"

"What I believe is that the reason you committed your crimes is directly related to the abuse you've suffered combined with symptoms of an untreated mental illness." Angela looked Jessica in the eye. "With that being said, you have some serious charges stacked up against you."

"Two charges of murder and one charge of attempted murder." Mary Ellen's death was ruled as accidental, so Jessica vowed that she would take that secret to the grave. There was no way they could prove she had anything to do with the poisoning. "They would *all* still be alive if they hadn't tried to ruin my life." She paused a moment before adding, "I know that I'm going to prison, but I just don't want to end up on death row."

"Once you speak to a psychiatrist to confirm what I believe is true—I'm sure the death penalty will be taken off the table," Angela said. "I really want you to consider taking a plea deal."

"You don't want a trial by jury. They may not be sympathetic."

Jessica dropped her head. Angela's statement was real, so there wasn't any other choice for her.

Chapter 52

Chrissy and Aiden entered the Chrystal ballroom at the downtown Radisson Hotel to attend a charity event to raise awareness for domestic violence on Saturday evening.

"I'm constantly learning new things about you," she said. "I had no idea that you were so involved with this cause."

"My stepfather used to beat my mother," Aiden said, pulling at his bowtie. "We left in the middle of the night when I was nine. Even though we moved from the Midwest to here… it was years before my mother stopped looking over her shoulder."

"I've been there," Chrissy said. "I was a magnet for abusive men when I was younger."

He stopped in his steps. "You?"

She nodded. "Right now, let's do our part for charity. We can talk later."

"Of course," Aiden replied.

Chrissy accepted a glass of wine from a passing waiter while Aiden requested a glass of sparkling water. "There are a lot of people here tonight. Is it always like this."

"It seems to grow in attendance each year."

They stopped to chat with a couple of his friends who had been invited to attend the silent auction and dinner.

On the way to their table, Aiden stopped to speak to a woman whom he introduced as a close friend of his mother's.

"Is there anyone here that you *don't* know?" Chrissy asked.

He gave her a gorgeous smile. "The only person I want to know is you. I think we've spent enough time together that you should be comfortable enough to let down that wall of yours."

"You're right. There are some things you need to know before we go any farther. That's what I want to talk about after we leave here."

"She's certainly shaking everything she's got," Chrissy said as she eyed a woman dancing to the music.

"Why don't we get out there and show her how it's really done?"

"My dancing days are over."

"Saved people can dance, too."

"I agree. It's my knees that are the problem. I've been having some problems with them."

Her heart quickened at the show of concern on his face.

"Do you mind if we leave?" she asked. "There's something I need to tell you."

"Sure."

"So here we are," Aiden said when they walked into her condo.

She smiled. "I've always told you that I will be honest with you. Before our relationship goes any further—there is something else that you should know."

"I'm listening."

"I'm bipolar. That's the first thing you need to know. I am seeing a therapist and taking medication."

"I know that you thought this information would have me running for the door." Aiden reached over and grabbed her hand. "I'm not going anywhere."

"There's more you need to know."

Aiden kissed her. "I know all that I need to know, sweetheart."

"Holt Deveraux is my brother."

"What?"

"Jessie Belle was my mother. She gave me and my sister up right after we were born."

"You have a twin sister?"

She nodded. "Her name is Jessica Campana... Jessica Ricks."

"The one that's been on the news."

Chrissy nodded. "She is the one in jail right now. You were out of town when she came here and I had her arrested."

"I have to admit I wasn't prepared for *this* information. Does Holt know about you?"

"Yes," Chrissy responded. "We have a relationship and it's good."

"What about your sister?"

"She only found out that we're twins the day she came here. Everyone believes that she would've killed me, but I don't. Jessica wanted her family, so she wouldn't have hurt me. I had her arrested because she needs help. Both of us suffered from our mother's abandonment and rejection—that's why I have to help her."

"I met her Pastor Deveraux a few months back at a brunch."

"Jessie Belle was not the nicest of people. Traynor, on the other hand is a sweetheart. He has stepped up and treats me like his own daughter."

"That's wonderful."

"I am so thankful to have him and Holt in my life." Chrissy pulled Aiden's face closer to her own. "I'm thrilled to have you in my life. I've never had any man treat me the way that you do. I'm thirty-five years old and I feel like a young girl in love for the first time."

"Is that your way of saying that you love me?"

Her eyes met his gaze straight on. "Yes."

Aiden kissed her.

"I need you to understand that I'm not going to abandon Jessica. She needs me."

"I can't say I agree with your decision, but I will support you."

"Thank you." She paused a moment before saying, "Now that you know all of this, I think it's time you met them."

He grinned. "So I'm finally meeting the family. Cool."

She laughed. "You're silly."

"Everyone, this is Aiden… my boyfriend," Chrissy announced shortly after they arrived to Holt's house. Everyone had gathered there for a family dinner.

After he was greeted by Traynor and Holt, Angela and Frankie hugged him.

"See… nothing to worry about," Chrissy whispered as they sat down in the family room.

"Chrissy is like a daughter to me, so I have to ask you," Traynor said, "what are your intentions toward her?"

"I eventually want to be introduced as her husband, sir. My intentions are to marry your daughter."

Frankie winked at Chrissy. "He's so honorable."

"You do know that I'm thirty-five years old, Traynor."

"And?"

She looked over at Aiden, then back at Traynor. "I… I'm glad you asked that question."

They all laughed.

Chrissy looked around the room. Everyone was talking and laughing. *So this is what it feels like to be part of a real family.* Her heart was full of indescribable emotion. At this moment, she felt that life simply couldn't get any better than this.

She thought of Jessica and her heart sank a little. Her sister should be here with them. Chrissy longed for the day when they could all be together. God was a God of miracles—he would make it so, she declared silently.

Chapter 53

"Are you ready?"

Jessica looked up. Angela looked great in her navy dress and jacket. Her shoes were a taupe color which matched her large tote. Her makeup was minimal and her hair pulled back in a bun. "Yes."

"This was delivered to my office by Clayton Ricks. He said he was your fiancé."

"Thank you." Though the change of clothes was for the benefit of the judge and district attorney, Jessie was thrilled to get out of the jumpsuit, even if only for a little while. "Clayton wants to marry me, but I can't think about marriage now."

"He made it clear that he loves you."

"I've never known love, but the way Clayton treats me... I imagine that's what it would feel like."

"Jessica, I don't want you to lose hope. You can't give up now."

"I'm not the one in control this time." She folded her arms across her chest. "I never should've come back to Raleigh, but I couldn't stay away. Revenge was like an addiction—I needed it."

"I'll see you in the courtroom."

Jessica tipped her chin up and looked at the fluorescent light fixtures—they were ugly. She took a deep cleansing breath and exhaled slowly.

She wanted to pray, but surely God would not listen to her now. He might forgive her, but she would have no choice in the consequences of her actions.

Minutes later, a guard escorted her down the long corridor filled with wooden double doors that led into courtrooms. It was here that her fate would be decided. Although she accepted a deal, the judge could throw it out in favor of a more severe punishment.

Jessica's eyes widened in surprise when she entered the courtroom to find Traynor, Holt and Chrissy present. Her gaze traveled to where Clayton was seated. She greeted him with a smile.

The double doors in the back of the room opened. In walked Natalia and Martha, both sending sharp daggers toward Jessica. She turned her attention to the front. The proceedings were due to start shortly.

Jessica chewed on her bottom lip and clasped her trembling hands together.

Angela leaned over and whispered, "It's going to work out."

She gave a slight nod.

The judge entered the room and sat down. The court reporter's hands were poised above her machine.

"I understand the defendant has accepted a plea deal,"

began the judge.

"Yes, your honor," the assistant District Attorney said. "Miss Ricks has agreed to serve a minimum sentence of ten years in prison for the murders of Michael and Charlotte Jennings, and six years for the attempted murders of Natalia Winters and Chrissy Barton. As part of the agreement, Miss Ricks has to undergo treatment for her mental illness. I spoke to Dr. Caleb Spencer, who is one of the country's foremost experts on borderline personality disorder. He faxed me a complete report on the ability of a person who suffers from this mental illness when they are threatened by outside influences like abandonment and abuse. He agrees with the previous psych evaluation."

"Is there anything the defendant would like to say?"

"Yes, your honor," Jessica said.

She rose to her feet.

"I made some terrible choices that landed me in this courtroom. All I've ever known was pain, but it was not my right to punish those I felt contributed to that pain. I fully understand the charges and the plea agreement I signed. I recognize now that I have a mental illness which greatly affected some of the decisions I made. I deeply regret hurting Mike, Charlotte and Natalia." Jessica turned to look at Martha and Natalia. "I am sorry for my actions."

From the expressions on their faces, they were clearly not moved by her words. She hadn't expected any other reaction. Forgiveness would not come from them.

Jessica looked over at Chrissy. "I'm so sorry."

When it was time for victim statements, Martha spoke first.

"My granddaughter lost her parents," she said. "I lost my daughter. There are no words to describe the pain I feel.

Charlotte didn't deserve this. Neither did her husband, despite his actions. Do I feel justice will be served by her spending sixteen years in prison? I would feel better if it were a life sentence because that's what she took from my daughter and Michael—their lives."

Jessica's hands curled into fists. She felt a surge of anger well up in her.

Angela scribbled something on a sheet of paper and passed it to her.

Breathe.

She hadn't realized that she was holding her breath. Jessica exhaled slowly and unfurled her hands.

Natalia spoke next.

"I do believe that the defendant is psychotic—she's a danger to society and I do not feel that sixteen years is enough. Like Martha, a life sentence is more appropriate. Not only did she try to kill me, she set fire to my house and most recently, tried to frame me for Charlotte and Mike's deaths. She is evil. She should never be allowed to roam free in the world."

Jessica kept her gaze on Natalia while she spoke. She refused to shrink down in her chair—she would face her victims straight on.

The last person to speak was Chrissy.

"Jessica committed heinous crimes. I understand the pain that Mrs. Adams and Natalia

Winters Anderson feel. I disagree that my sister should be locked up for the rest of her life. If a person has not walked in her shoes—it is not easy to accept that her actions were colored by the abandonment by our mother, by the physical and verbal abuse she suffered, and being raped by the man she thought was her father—this man got her pregnant at fourteen. The loss of that child only added to her pain." Chrissy's eyes watered.

"I understand Jessica's agony because my life was just as bad. I felt enraged when our birth mother wanted nothing to do with me. Like my sister, I wanted to be part of a loving family. I yearned to know what it would be like. I want to be clear—what my sister did was wrong. Jessica and I are twins. I am bipolar and I've done things that I regret. I pray that your honor will express leniency by accepting the plea deal and allowing my sister to get the treatment that she needs. I also ask the she be placed in a minimum-security facility close by so that we can provide her with the family support she needs. I believe being near her family will aid in her rehabilitation."

Jessica sat staring at Chrissy in disbelief.

"Jessica Belle Ricks, would you please stand," the judge said.

She moved her chair back with her legs, and then rose to her feet.

"Before I render my decision, I want to go on record saying that while I believe the defendant should serve the maximum number of years allowed for her actions, I cannot ignore the facts surrounding her mental state. According to the psychiatrist's report, the defendant's pain is so internalized that she's numb on the outside, disturbing her ability to make decisions or react based on emotion. With this in mind, I will accept the plea agreement, but I am going to add an additional four years' probation."

Epilogue

Five Years Later

As soon as Jessica stepped outside into the prison yard. Her eyes filled with tears. Her psychiatrist had convinced the warden that allowing her an hour with her family would add to her treatment.

During her time in the prison, Jessica had taken classes in psychology and obtained a degree. She was now working on a Master's degree. Her initial interest in this field of science was because she wanted to know more about her disorder.

Chrissy rushed to her side and embraced her. "I told you that we would be here. *Happy Birthday.*"

She smiled. "Same to you, twin."

Chrissy had been true to her word. She wrote letters, mailed Jessica motivational books and music. Holt wrote letters and sent her care packages as well. In truth, they were the reason she could get through the days and nights.

"We brought you gifts, but the guards said they had to inspect them."

Jessica nodded. "I painted you a picture." She handed it to Chrissy.

"Is this us?"

"Yeah. The way it should have been."

Chrissy's eyes grew wet. "It's not too late. I love it, Jess."

She chuckled. "It's corny."

"I still love it."

"Did you give the letters to Natalia & Martha?"

Chrissy nodded. "You apologized and asked them to forgive you—you've done your part."

"I'm not expecting to hear anything back." Jessica shrugged. "It's fine, though."

Traynor walked over to her. "Happy Birthday, Jessica."

"Thank you... thank you for everything."

"No looking back," he said. "Only forward."

"I'm teaching Bible study this coming Tuesday," Jessica announced. "We take turns each week."

"That's wonderful."

"Angela seems to make you very happy," Jessica said. "I'm glad."

"She's a good woman."

"You're a good man, Traynor. "Perhaps if I had been raised by you... things would've turned out differently."

He smiled. "God is not done with you, Jessica. Your testimony is going to change lives. Even in here."

"A few years ago, I would've laughed at you, but I know that you're right," she responded. "Whenever I get out, I want to work with female inmates."

Traynor embraced her. "But God..."

Jessica joined the others at the picnic table.

"I made those cookies you love," Frankie said. "Your brother tried to go into them, but I wouldn't let him."

"He could've had one."

Holt frowned. "Just *one*."

She nodded. "Those cookies get me through those long papers I have to write."

"I guess I can't argue with that."

"Okay honey, I'll just make a double batch," Frankie said. "How about that?"

He grinned.

Jessica and Chrissy looked at one another before laughing.

"What?"

"You are so spoiled," Chrissy said.

"Hey, my wife loves me."

Chrissy and Jessica took a walk around the basketball court.

"You don't have to worry about me. I'm never going back down that dark road again."

"I'm so proud of you, Jessica."

"Thank you for being so supportive. I don't know if I'd made it without you and Holt."

"I never thought these words would come out of my mouth, but I love you."

"Wow…"

"I know… awkward…"

"Sis, I love you, too."

Wiping her eyes, Chrissy said, "Let's go back and join the others."

"Wait…" Jessica stated. "Do you really believe that I can do this? Do you believe I can leave here and build a normal life after all that I've done?"

"Yes," Chrissy responded. "You won't have to do it alone. You have a family, but most importantly, I have faith."

As they headed back to the picnic area, Chrissy asked, "How are things between you and Clayton?"

"He's back in New York, but he visits me once a month. He is still asking me to marry him."

"What did you tell him?"

"There are things that you don't know about Clayton."

"I know that he's X in your journal. You two have been through a lot together. I also suspect that his job has something to do with narcotics."

Jessica glanced around to see if anyone was close enough to hear their conversation.

"It's not really a secret," Chrissy said. "We all figured as much. Jess, I know that he loves you, but the life he leads… it's not something you want or need to be involved with."

"He is talking about letting go all of that stuff. Clayton says that he sees how much I've changed and the way you all stuck by me… he thinks I have a great family. He says he's been going to church. He has a lot of questions, so I told him to talk to the pastor. We were never exposed to anything spiritual growing up."

"Better late than never." Chrissy stared at her. "I still can't get over the fact that you had eye implant surgery. What were you thinking?"

"I don't really know," Jessica responded. "All I can say is that we do some crazy things out of perceived desperation. I've heard some horror stories and I'm grateful that I haven't had any problems."

"Thank goodness for that."

Jessica nodded in agreement.

"Have the nightmares stopped?"

Jessica shook her head. "Now that my mind is much clearer, the things I've done—they weigh heavy on me." She looked at Chrissy. "There's something you all deserve to know." Mary Ellen's death still haunted her and she wanted to unburden herself.

"Did you lay it before the Lord and repent?"

"Y-Yes." Tears threatened to spill from her eyes.

"Then leave it there, Jess. Keep it between you and God."

She wiped her eyes. "The best thing to come out of all this is that I have you and Holt."

"And I have sisters," he said from behind them. "Our time is almost up, so c'mon and eat."

"I'm not hungry," Jessica said. "All I want to do is cherish this time. I've never had a birthday party so I need pictures. Oh, and I'm not wearing that stupid party hat."

Holt grinned. "Yes, you are."

Chrissy laughed.

"Why are you laughing?" Frankie asked. "I have one for you, too."

"No, this is Jessica's first party—I want this to be all about her."

"You're not getting off that easy. If I have to wear one, so do you."

Frankie took photos of the siblings alone and then with Traynor and Angela.

When they prepared to leave, Jessica said, "Thank you for today."

"Chrissy will mail you the photos," Frankie promised.

"Oh, Aiden wanted you to know that he would've been here but he had to go to Toronto for a month."

"How is married life?"

Chrissy grinned. "More wonderful than I could ever imagine. In fact, we're adopting a little boy and his sister. We didn't want to separate them."

"That's wonderful news."

"When you come home, I'll give you back your journal."

"The first thing I'm going to do is destroy it. I don't need it anymore."

Back in her cell, Jessica waited until the guard walked away before she burst into tears.

Watching her family leave without her was never an easy thing to do. It was a reminder that she'd taken the wrong path to finding her family. She was comforted that despite everything, they had chosen to stand by her side. There were times when Jessica felt it would have been less painful if they had not. Her thirst for revenge could have led to her destruction, but instead it became her salvation.

Wiping her eyes, Jessica picked up her Bible. Whenever she read the Word, she was in awe of the magnitude of God's love for imperfect people, even a murderer. The Ten Commandments stated it clearly: *You shall not murder.*

Five years ago, it was still hard for Jessica to accept that God could forgive her grievous sins, but then the prison chaplain explained that there was only one sin that God would not forgive—the sin of refusing His forgiveness. The chaplain told her about the time Jesus Christ forgave a murderer.

Saul of Tarsus hated Christians and was responsible for sending many of them to their death. He was forgiven and his life changed—Saul became the Apostle Paul, the greatest Christian who ever lived. It was Paul's journey that encouraged and gave Jessica hope that through God's love for her, she would find her redemption.

The Jezebel Series

Jezebel

Jezebel's Daughter

Jezebel's Revenge

Coming Summer 2017

CPSIA information can be obtained
at www.ICGtesting.com
Printed in the USA
LVOW11s1502040117
519724LV00001B/106/P